First published in Great Britain in 2018

First Linford Edition
published 2020

A catalogue record for this book is available
from the British Library.

ISBN 978–1–4448–4531–0

Published by
Ulverscroft Limited
Anstey, Leicestershire

Set by Words & Graphics Ltd.
Anstey, Leicestershire
Printed and bound in Great Britain by
T. J. International Ltd., Padstow, Cornwall

This book is printed on acid-free paper

ALAN C. WILLIAMS

RETURN TO TASMANIA

Complete and Unabridged

LINFORD
Leicester

Books by Alan C. Williams
in the Linford Romance Library:

CHRISTMAS DOWN UNDER
LOST IN THE OUTBACK
SEARCHING FOR SCARLETT

RETURN TO TASMANIA

Heading back from Sydney to her idyllic childhood home in Tasmania, Sandie's priorities are to recover from a bullet wound, reconsider her future in the police, and spend time with her sister and niece. But even as the plane lands, she senses that a fellow passenger is not all he seems. When a series of suspicious events follow her arrival, the mystery man reveals himself as Adam, who has been sent to protect Sandie's family as they become embroiled in the fall-out following the double-crossing of a dangerous criminal.

1

As the plane flew towards its destination at Hobart, I peered out of the window once more.

It was amazing that the Midlands were so dry this early in the summer. The rolling fields were a golden oatmeal scene below us with the occasional white dot of a sheep. It reminded me of how harsh some parts of Tassie were and how some things would never change, despite it only being three days to the millennium.

I shifted uncomfortably in my seat. My left arm was aching so much I reached for a codeine tablet in the top pocket of my blouse. The doctor in Sydney had advised me of the maximum dose and I was reluctant to exceed that, despite the pain. I popped the blister packet back in my pocket.

'You OK, miss?' the man on my right asked. He hadn't spoken to me before

on the long flight from Sydney. I felt sorry for him being squished in the middle seat as he was a little on the tubby side. He'd drawn short straw as his wife apparently needed to stretch her legs out into the aisle. He didn't have much room for his size.

Unfortunately, the plane was packed. Maybe that was why I'd been bumped from yesterday's flight. Probably loads of tourists visiting in order to experience the finish of the yearly Sydney to Hobart Yacht Race.

'Yes, thanks,' I replied with a forced smile. I hated flying, especially when total strangers were so close that they invaded my personal space.

He seemed pleasant enough, a little intimidated by his overbearing wife. Mid to late sixties, balding with his remaining hair and bushy moustache the colour of snow. His eyes, though tired, were kind. I often judged people by their eyes, despite being advised not to throughout my training.

'Name's Bill. Bill Eastman. This is

my missus, Val.' He indicated his wife who nodded politely.

I felt obliged to stick with the pleasantries and reply. Perhaps talking would take my mind off the dull ache. Well not so dull, actually.

'Sandie Ashton. Pleased to meet you both.'

'Your first time in Tasmania?' Bill asked.

'No. I was born and raised here.'

His wife nudged him. I heard her whisper, 'Ask her.' Clearly there was something troubling them.

Bill turned to me. 'Will . . . will we have any problems with the locals understanding us?'

I smiled. Even in 1999, Mainlanders were still in the Dark Ages when it came to Australia's island state.

'No worries. Everyone speaks English here.'

'As well as Tasmanian?'

'I'm afraid someone's been winding you up. We're the same as other Aussies. A bit more laid back, that's all.

We don't have two heads, either.'

Another misconception — although I had seen teddy bears in a tourist shop in Ross where the teddies *did* have two heads. I'd thought it was a bit sick but most Mainlanders could see the joke, not realising it was on them.

Mr and Mrs Tourist seemed relieved. I returned to staring at the view. Why was I going back?

I guessed Tassie was still my home, my safe place. Heaven knows I needed that now. As well as discovering that my now ex-boyfriend wasn't actually divorced, I'd had a big wake-up call, a situation that shattered whatever self-confidence I had left. Now I was slinking home to my big sis like a dingo with her tail between her legs. I didn't expect any *I told you so* but in my thoughts, it was an admission of defeat; of not being able to cope.

Mum and Dad were overseas gallivanting as usual. We weren't talking much these days. More so, since I chose not to follow Dad into the scientific

community he adored so much.

My parents' marriage hadn't been a bed of roses and I was often caught in the middle. Dad was one of those fathers who always wanted to be in control — though, in spite of some hiccups on the way, I was now my own person.

Quite simply I was going to Paula because I didn't have anyone else. Being focussed on my career did have its downside . . . especially when I didn't know if I could ever return to it.

When Dad had been promoted twelve years ago, I'd gone with my parents to Sydney, leaving my older sis in Hobart. I was fourteen. I had no choice. In spite of growing up in Sydney and going to school and Uni there, it was never home.

Paula was supposed to meet me at the airport and I was looking forward to seeing her and Lauren once again. Paula was six years older than I. We'd never been that close; the occasional phone call and a visit every few years. She seemed content, regardless of having what I thought was a mundane, boring life.

I'd rung her from hospital last week. She seemed surprised to hear from me before our normal Christmas Day phone call. When I told her what had happened, she immediately suggested that I stay with her.

I'd been so relieved, I started blubbering. Not my usual self at all. She'd offered to come to Sydney to fetch me but I still had some pride. Physically it was only my shoulder. Mentally? Well, that was another matter. I hoped that being with her would help me get my brain back together.

As we began to descend, we hit an air pocket. I bashed my arm against the cabin wall. I swore as a spasm of pain ripped through my body. The stitches weren't a problem but it hurt so much.

Mr and Mrs Tourist were staring at me in shock, obviously uncomfortable with young ladies using language like that. I swivelled around so that they could see my left shoulder as I lifted the short sleeve of my floral blouse. They stared at the bandages.

'Sorry about the language. Had an op on my arm last week. I hurt it quite severely.'

They offered their platitudes, asking if there was anything they could do.

'Thanks. Could you call the stewardess? I need a drink. Brandy, please. And dry ginger.'

I fumbled for the tablets and swallowed two as the stewardess returned with the drinks.

Medication and alcohol don't mix, I recalled the doc telling me.

Stuff that, I thought as I downed the mixture in one gulp. *And stuff the so-and-so who did this to me and my life.*

* * *

We landed soon afterwards at Hobart International Airport. It was a standing joke among Taswegians — a term some Mainlanders used. The only destinations planes flew to, or from, were cities on the mainland of Oz. Disused signs

7

for Passport Control still adorned the empty end where planes used to fly to New Zealand. Now Hobart was a small, regional airport; no jet-setters heading off to Asia or Europe.

We taxied to a stop on the apron outside the terminal building. Our Qantas jet was the only commercial plane in sight. Some things in Tassie never changed.

The painkillers were kicking in. *Welcome home, Sandie*, I thought.

'What do you plan to do while you're here?' I asked Mr Tourist as I unbuckled my seat belt.

'Check out the yachts from the big race. Do some sightseeing. Port Arthur, the west coast, Launceston and Wine Glass Bay. We want to see it all.'

'And how long are you staying?'

'Three days,' Mrs Tourist responded. Her sparkly glasses reminded me of Dame Edna's.

Good luck with that, I thought. Tassie was half the size of England; sixty-odd thousand square kilometres. I

couldn't imagine anyone expecting to see England in six days, but maybe they'd expect that too if they ever went there.

In retrospect, I was being too harsh. I'd been to the UK on a training course this year. I guess I was pretty ignorant of its size at the time, expecting to drive from London to Liverpool in an hour.

'Tassie's a big place, Bill and Val. Perhaps Hobart one day, Port Arthur the next and Wine Glass Bay on the third.'

We stood ready to disembark. I glanced around at the other passengers. There were families with excited kiddies, quite a few elderly people like Val and Bill, tourists and locals coming home as well as a few suits . . . business types. I noted them all, making instant assumptions about relationships, ages and occupations. It was second nature and I couldn't switch that part of my life off.

Most people notice a few cursory details about strangers. Maybe hair

9

colour and age, if that. Not me. If I were to close my eyes I could recite specific details about all the people on our plane, from the thirtysomething bloke in a charcoal grey suit with Paisley tie to his older male companion with the yellowing teeth and ill-fitting hairpiece.

Some would regard that as a gift; others a curse. I'd seen that Mrs Tourist had two passports in her royal blue handbag. No doubt they'd been told they needed them, probably by the same joker who told them Tassies spoke some foreign language. She also had an aqua glasses case, a glittery purse and hairbrush with strands of grey hairs. Obviously she'd recently had her hair done for the special holiday here as it was now a chestnut brown. I'd only seen inside her handbag for a few seconds. It had been enough.

As passengers queued to disembark, reaching into their overhead lockers for luggage and coats, one bloke caught my attention. Cropped black hair and casual

clothing, but definitely no tourist. Mystery Man was someone pretending to be different than he was. He was totally wrong.

He was staring back at me, like some animal suspecting a predator nearby. He smiled enigmatically. I sensed he was a predator too.

He was less than three metres away, close enough to see the unusual combination of azure blue eyes with his hair colouring. His gaunt face was dark from the beard that was only hours old. Inwardly I shivered. The French call it a frisson; a sensation of fear or excitement. In his case it was certainly disquieting. Although there was no reason for me to feel that way, I trusted my instincts implicitly.

Hopefully he was going elsewhere. I didn't need this in my life, not after last week.

He didn't break eye contact as most people did when caught staring. Evidently the rules of polite behaviour weren't for him, just as they didn't

apply to me. Instead he hoisted his small bag off the seat and began to move to the forward exit, stopping only to permit me to step out from between my rows of seats, ahead of him.

I hesitated, waving him past.

'You first, Miss. I insist.' His voice sounded polite and warm. Another deception. He was taking charge of the situation, deliberately putting me at a disadvantage. Rather than cause a fuss, I nodded my thanks. Two could play this game.

I could feel his gaze on me as I began to shuffle down the aisle.

'Excuse me. You forgot your jacket,' I heard him say. I turned to face him as he lifted my jacket from the seat where I'd deliberately left it. I wanted to see him up close.

He was taller than I, about one metre eighty-five, mid-thirties, tanned and muscular with no excess fat. His brown slacks and khaki shirt were new, the packaging creases on his shirt obvious.

'Thanks,' I said with a quick smile.

12

'I'm so absent-minded.'

'I doubt that . . . Sandie.' I felt another cold shiver. How did he know my name?

As if reading my thoughts, he fingered the boarding card sticking out of my jacket pocket.

What was he doing? Flirting? No, this was far more sinister. My painful shoulder reminded me that I was in no position to challenge him.

I hurried from the exit and down the steps onto the windy Tarmac. It was important I put some space between us, regardless of the appearance that I was on the defensive. He'd unnerved me, big time, and I hated that.

I'd already had so much taken from me. Even here, on my home territory, I still felt vulnerable.

Walking briskly to the terminal building, I was conscious that the captain's suggestion to wear our coats was quite good advice. Even though it was four on a late December afternoon, Hobart was only a bracing fifteen degrees, far cooler

13

than the heatwave we'd left behind in Sydney. Tassie was Australia's southern most state after all. Next stop, going south, was Antarctica.

We were funnelled into the processing area. Large signs proclaimed that Tasmania was a quarantine state; there was a lengthy list of seafood, fruit and vegetable prohibited items as well as animal products. Our iconic Tassie sniffer dog with his handler moved between the passengers, checking for contraband.

Most people thought the beagle was cute, not regarding the situation as critical. I knew differently. Tassie's export industry depended on rules like these being obeyed. Possibly if they replaced the doggie with a more intimidating Tasmanian devil, tourists would be more wary of inadvertently smuggling foodstuffs in. On second thoughts, people being savaged by a sniffer devil might not be good for much-needed tourism.

Mystery Man was about six people

behind me. Was I being paranoid, or suffering the effects of the alcohol? I thought not. My training and instincts said otherwise.

We exited into the small meet-and-greet hall. I looked around; Paula should have been here. Other arriving passengers embraced friends or relatives or made their way to the car-hire desks.

Mystery Man passed me, heading to the gents. He returned moments later. Now he was making a point of totally ignoring me and although it seemed convincing, I suspected otherwise. He made a call on a mobile phone as I collected my tapestry suitcase from the baggage reclaim. It was hard to lift it off with one hand so an airport employee helped me out.

The concourse was emptying and the carousel ground to a halt. Still no sign of Paula.

Finally I saw a familiar figure dashing across from the car park. She had a young girl by her side. Surely it

couldn't be Lauren! She'd grown. She must be seven — no, eight, recalling the last card and pressie I'd sent.

'Apologies, Sandie,' my out-of-breath sister said, moving in to hug me until I reminded her of my arm. A half-hug still felt good.

'And who's this grown-up young lady? Surely it can't be my favourite niece.'

Lauren giggled at our little game. 'I'm your only niece, Auntie Sandie. Thanks heaps for my Christmas gift. It's really cool.'

I looked over to Paula. Obviously she bought one on my behalf knowing I was in hospital. Thinking about the proper one in my luggage, I prayed she'd think that one 'really cool' too.

'Too old for a welcome kiss?' I asked, crouching down. 'Just watch my arm.'

My niece had certainly grown. Her long, golden ponytail suited her and that cheeky grin reminded me of myself way back when. By contrast, though, she wore a pretty cerise dress, unlike

the dirty jeans and tattered shirts I used to prefer. She obviously took after her demurely-dressed mum.

'No way, Auntie.' She returned my embrace, carefully. 'Does your arm hurt much? What happened? Mum told me you had to be in hospital. Were the doctors dishy?'

'Whoa, young lady. You're as nosy as your mum. It does hurt, but only a little. I . . . er . . . fell over on a piece of wood with rusty nails in it.'

That explanation would suit. I preferred that as few people as possible knew what had actually happened. In Tassie, that meant Paula but no one else. I didn't want Lauren getting upset.

'And yes, I was in hospital but there were no dishy doctors. In fact they were all yukky ugly,' I joked, pulling a face.

Paula stood back to check me out.

'Let's have a good look at my little sister. Still as scruffy as ever, I see. That hair. You're as bad as a cockatoo with it sticking up all over.'

'I like it short. Easier to manage,' I

replied, giving it a cursory pat. 'And I happen to like cockatoos . . . apart from their screeching.'

Paula's hair was immaculately styled in spite of the breeze outside. Her make-up was perfect. Same old Paula. Same old me.

'We're going to have a great time, Sandie. It's fantastic to have you here.'

'Thanks for putting me up, big sis. How come you were late?'

'I was on my way when I had to go back for Lauren. Bazza was supposed to collect her from dance lessons but didn't turn up. He hasn't answered my calls, either. I had to drive back to North Hobart to collect her. It's very unlike him.'

I didn't comment. I'd never taken to Paula's ex, even before they married. Now they were divorced I liked him less. Nevertheless, Paula defended him as Lauren's dad. It had always seemed that Barry had had another agenda for marrying my sister — almost as if he'd been coerced into it.

'I wonder what happened to him, Mum. You don't think he's hurt or anything?'

Paula cuddled her daughter, giving me a concerned glance.

'Of course not, sweetheart. Dad probably forgot or something silly. Come on. Let's get Auntie Sandie's bags. Pizza night tonight.'

Lauren clapped her hands. 'I love pizza.'

I began to lift my suitcase but fortunately Paula stepped in, taking it from me. We paid for the parking and headed outside. It was late afternoon.

'Sandie. Next time get one with wheels,' she remarked halfway back to her car, clearly struggling with the weight.

I felt a touch guilty. Paula wasn't as strong as I was. Maybe I'd gone overboard with my packing.

I recalled Mr Tall, Dark and Creepy back in the terminal. I wondered if I'd cross paths again with him again. Despite Tassie's size, every day I'd

probably meet someone from my past. Lots of space but surprisingly few inhabitants.

At that moment my sister's mobile rang.

'It's Bazza. Hello ... Where were you? I had to — Hold on, Bazza. I don't understand. You'll what? In a few days? Bazza? Bazza? ... ' She hung up, clearly upset. 'That was — '

'Barry. We know.' I gave Lauren a reassuring smile, noticing that, like her mum, she was becoming agitated. Fortunately Paula noticed my efforts and was suddenly all smiles for her girl.

'Was that Dad? Is something wrong?'

'No, sweetheart. Nothing's wrong. Dad was ringing to say he's sorry he couldn't collect you from dance. He had an emergency at work.'

'Oh,' said Lauren, seemingly satisfied. She skipped across the empty walkway to Paula's car as we both hung back.

'Something up with Mr Wonderful?' I asked.

I sensed Paula was about to say something protective, yet she paused. She still had feelings for him; he was Lauren's father, after all. However she was concerned and I was the obvious confidant. She kept her voice down.

'He told me that he needed to disappear for a few days. He was — I don't think I'm imagining it, Sandie — he seemed on edge. Said he was turning his phone off, hence not to ring him. He'd contact me at work once things had settled down and not to worry.'

I put my good arm around her, reassuringly.

'If he said not to worry, then don't. I'm sure there's a simple explanation.'

Paula nodded. 'If anyone can handle himself, it's Bazza. All that Army training, I guess.'

We walked to Paula's Verada where Lauren was waiting. I hated to lie to Paula but, just as she'd calmed Lauren, I needed to comfort her. I had the impression Barry was hiding from

21

someone, and had probably removed his sim card as well as turning his phone off the moment he'd hung up.

I suspected he was in trouble. I only hoped whatever mess he was embroiled in, wouldn't affect Paula or Lauren as well.

2

Conversation on the drive towards Hobart was subdued. I told Lauren I had a headache from my injured arm and didn't feel up to talking. Happily she accepted that, sitting back on the seat behind me. She seemed content to play some puzzle game by herself. My headache excuse wasn't far from the truth.

In addition, the alcohol had been a bad idea. Being the ripe old age of twenty-six didn't mean I was immune from making stupid decisions.

Paula's car was quite roomy, one of the more luxurious models on the market. She explained her choice as a bit of class to impress the clients she drove around. She'd started her own real estate business a few years before, buying and selling houses as well as rentals. In truth, my big sis wanted the

car as a decadent whim for herself. She loved the better things in life.

'Dollar for your thoughts, kid,' Paula said.

'A dollar?'

'Inflation,' she replied with a laugh.

I pointed at the spectacular landscape ahead of us; Hobart standing proudly on the other side of the Derwent River. To the left, we could see the Wrest Point Casino, a cylindrical tower standing on the river shore, straight ahead the Tasman Bridge joining Hobart to the eastern suburbs. Behind our capital, like some imposing guardian, Mount Wellington dwarfed my former home.

'Don't tell me there's snow up there. It's the end of December,' I said, pointing.

'We've had a cold spring. Tomorrow's supposed to be twenty-five, though.' Paula loved Tassie and was a great ambassador for those often elderly Aussies who decided to spend their twilight years down here by purchasing a new home.

'Yeah. A Tassie twenty-five. Pretty

24

hot.' I knew from experience that, due to the diminished ozone layer above us, we could very easily get sunburned at temperatures most other Australians would regard as cool.

'Just wondering about the next few days,' I continued, answering her earlier query. 'I'm on leave for a few weeks at least. Nothing to do but recuperate and enjoy being back in paradise with you guys. I'll do whatever you want — babysitting, for a start?'

'I'm not a baby!' Lauren called indignantly from the back seat. I turned my head, grinning.

'Just checking you were awake back there.'

Paula made a suggestion she'd obviously been considering for a while.

'Actually I'd prefer you to help out at work. We're a bit short-staffed. That is, if you can manage it? You were always a whizzkid with accounts.'

'What about my beautiful niece? School hols?'

'All sorted. She's doing the next two

days at Bellevue Cricket Club. It's a programme to encourage girls to take up the game. David Boon will be there.'

I was impressed. Boonie was one of those larger-than-life Aussie cricketers born and raised in Tassie just like we were.

'And then I'll be staying with Great-Gran and Grandad for a week,' Lauren chirped in.

In contrast to the relationship disasters that had plagued our parents and us, our mother's parents were one of marriage's success stories. Maybe it was modern-day life that was simply too hectic for a stable love bond to exist, I mused.

'How are they?' I asked, nonchalantly. I felt guilty about how I'd treated them over the years.

'Brilliant. They're keen to see you again. Thought we'd head down on Sunday to drop Lauren off. Gran has a new tractor.'

Our grandparents had a very topsy-turvy lifestyle. She preferred to look

after the extensive gardens and related machinery while Grandad did the cooking and housework.

'What? She's sixty-five. Guess she must be doing OK.'

We were on the Bridge. I tensed a little at the thought of how high we were, trying not to look over the side. Planes were fine, but for some reason other high places made me anxious. And then there was the memory of what happened immediately after I was hurt. I could still see the terror on his face as he fell to the waters below . . .

I pushed those bad thoughts to the back of my mind. I was here to get my head back together. 'Right you two,' I said, trying to feel positive. 'What pizza are we getting for our takeaway? Pavlova too. My treat.'

Lauren gave a squeal of delight. 'Yay.'

⋆　⋆　⋆

I'd stayed in Paula's riverside unit before. It was spacious and beautifully

27

decorated. By comparison, my own unit near the beach was a tip. I simply wasn't a home person.

After Paula tucked Lauren into bed, I read her some of the latest Harry Potter book, *The Prisoner Of Azkaban*. It had just come out when I was in Liverpool, England, and I'd sent it for Lauren's birthday. Paula had told me she was a big fan.

Later, Paula opened a bottle of Pinot Noir from one of the local wineries. I chose to stick to a soft drink. My arm was usually worse in the evening.

We chatted until about nine. The sun was setting and the light on the river was so serene.

'What happened to you made the news, down here,' she said out of the blue.

I was surprised. Mainland news was not usually a high point of telly reports in Tasmania.

'Do you want to talk about it?' she asked.

I thought about it for a few seconds.

Was I ready to share the horrific details with my closest family?

'Not yet. But I know you'll be there when I am. To be truthful, it wasn't my finest hour.'

Paula reached over, placing her hands on mine.

'It's fine to admit you're not Wonder Woman all the time, you know.'

I grinned, recalling the super-heroine cossie I wore at home for months when I was about Lauren's age. Paula laughed a little.

'We've still got that outfit at Gran's, tucked away in a trunk somewhere.'

'Might be a bit tight for me these days. How about Lauren?'

'She's more into elegant princesses and brave knights, I'm afraid,' said Paula indicating some of the photos on the wall.

I sighed. 'Probably more sensible. Wonder Womaning isn't all it's cracked up be. And the way I feel right now, I'd prefer to live my life as an unassuming nobody than any super-heroine.'

29

'You might not go back to that job, then?'

'We'll have to wait and see, big sis. But right now I don't think I could ever do that again.'

* ★ ★

The following morning, after dropping Lauren at her sports course, we drove to Paula's office. She confessed that finances were fairly tight, having lost some potential big sales and sole agencies to the opposition, Mandeville Real Estate.

I was introduced to her team. There was Holly Rockford, a youthful, engaging receptionist who also ran the rental department, and another salesperson, Yvonne Lawson.

'Summer's a busy time listing and selling houses. Holly's already sent out the end of month statements to our rental property owners and arranged payments. She's bright and everyone likes her. I'd appreciate you just helping

out, especially with accounts.'

'Yeah. No problem. It'll be something to keep my mixed-up mind occupied.'

'It's not as if you need to be here all the time. You can go shopping or wander around whenever you want. Sandy Bay's got some great eating places.'

I winced. How long would it be before someone made a smart comment, *Fancy that, a woman called Sandie in Sandy Bay.*

'Yeah. About that, Paula. Why Sandy Bay?'

I brushed some lint off my dress. Paula insisted I try to look professional even though I was an unpaid dogsbody. I preferred slacks and a loose blouse; more comfortable. As for the high heeled shoes . . .

'Sandy Bay's quite upmarket and, at the time I set up shop, I thought we'd do well here. Lately, I'm not so sure. We lost another of our rental landlords to the opposition this morning.'

'Is that important?'

31

'The rental charges are our steady income, our bread and butter. Commissions for selling can fluctuate month to month. I'd like you to sit in with Holly and get a feel for the accounts. She'll show you the books.'

I stared at her. 'Books? You're not using a computer programme like MYOB; Mind Your Own Business?' Although my job in Sydney didn't involve accounting programmes, I felt it was important to keep up to date with my original choice of profession. Right now, I was seriously considering it once more.

'Holly is more familiar with the traditional system. She's keen to try computer programmes but it's expensive to set up. Maybe next year? Mid next year. In the meantime, I trust her to keep on top of things. The last bloke wasn't much good.'

I felt uneasy. Mulder in *The X-Files* telly show summed it up as far as I was concerned — *Trust no one*. My big sis wouldn't last long in the big cities. Tassie was stuck back in the Seventies,

struggling along in its own little time warp. There were possibly still *discos* out there.

I remembered being like that when a Mainlander girl turned up at school once. It didn't help her case when she started singing that song *Sandy* from Grease whenever I was around, taunting me with Olivia Newton-John's innocence. We ended up trading blows and pulling hair. Dad told me off about unladylike behaviour. It was the start of my rebellion against him.

I spent the morning with Holly, getting a feel for her quaint accounting systems. She was an absolute joy to be around. Her long copper hair seemed to have a life of its own, flouncing around as she turned her constantly smiling face to visitors entering the office. Even her phone calls bubbled with enthusiasm. For a twenty-year-old just starting out, I could see why Paula thought she was an asset.

'She's bright, too,' my sister confided, watching her through the glass door of

her office. 'She's passed the Real Estate exams first time. As a rental manager, she's brill.'

By contrast, Yvonne seemed positively surly. Everything was a chore to her. She was about thirty-five, wearing a dull green dress that seemed to reflect her dour attitude. She was pretty enough, her hair and face reminding me of the dark-haired girl from Abba.

Basically the salespeople were paid on commission; one percent of the selling price if they sold the house and one percent if they listed it. The office took the other two percent.

I didn't mention my earlier run-in with Yvonne to Paula. Without warning she'd pounced, telling me she was top cat around the office and if I had any thoughts of coming to work for my sister as a saleswoman, she'd make my life untenable.

No, Yvonne was a proper little witch with a 'b' where the 'w' is. I'd backed down right away, countering her temper and flared nostrils with an explanation

close to the truth; I was on leave from my work in the Sydney following an accident. I showed her my bandaged arm and she settled down. As if the loud-mouthed harridan had any say in whom Paula chose to employ!

It was then that I realised then how much I'd changed since the incident the previous week. No way would the old me have put up with her attitude if I'd met her in downtown Sydney.

Yvonne looked over to Paula and me, nodding politely with a forced smile. I waved back. Her time would come — at least, I hoped so. All I needed was for my self-confidence to return.

Holly buzzed through from the front desk.

'Excuse me, boss. There are two uniformed police officers here. Shall I send them in?'

Instantly, I bristled with anger.

'Hell. Can't they leave me alone?'

Paula tried to calm me down. 'Does anyone know you're in this office? Not just in Tassie.'

I considered that point. 'No. I guess not.'

'Sometimes it's not all about you, Sandie. Let's see what they want first before ruffling those cockatoo feathers any more.'

I sighed, patting my hair. Paula was always the logical thinker of the two of us.

My sister pressed the intercom button. 'Could you show them in please, Holly? Thanks.'

I backed up into a corner of the office, leaning against a filing cabinet, arms crossed defiantly.

Paula stood up and smiled as they entered.

'Ms Ashton?' Paula had reverted to her maiden name after the divorce and had changed Lauren's surname too as she retained custody. 'I'm Sergeant Mick Nolan and this is Constable Jill Isherwood. We're trying to trace your ex-husband but he doesn't appear to be at home or at work . . .'

'And he's turned off his mobile,' the young policewoman added. Her sergeant gave her a disapproving look. She

stood back, clasping her hands diffidently in front of her immaculate uniform and bowed her head. Despite my feelings for uniformed cops, I had to suppress a smile. The eagerness of youth.

'I don't have any clue as to his whereabouts, Sergeant. He contacted me yesterday arvo to say he was going away for a while. There was no answer when I tried to ring him last night. What's it about, anyway? The burglary at his factory?'

My ears pricked up. 'What burglary, Paula?'

She turned to me. 'Over Christmas. They stole a lot of expensive equipment and computers. All the employees were questioned and fingerprinted to make sure it wasn't an inside job.'

The baby-faced Sergeant cleared his throat.

'And you are?'

Paula introduced me. 'My sister. From Sydney. Sandie Ashton.'

The policewoman laughed, despite herself. 'Sandie Ashton in Sandy Bay. Cool.'

Another stern glance, this time from both the sergeant and me. 'Sorry Sarge. Sorry, Miss Ashton.'

The policeman continued, 'We caught the thieves and recovered the stolen items. We wanted to see Mr Denvers on another matter. To help us with our enquiries. However it appears he's gone missing.'

'Perhaps he's a victim of the Tassie Triangle, Sarge?'

The senior police officer had had enough.

'I apologise for Constable Isherwood. It's her first week at the station; and possibly her last.'

'But Sarge . . . '

'It's Sergeant, thank you. Tassie Triangle, indeed. You've got the brains of a petrified wombat, Constable.' The young officer broke into a huge grin. 'That wasn't a compliment, Constable Isherwood. Wait for me in the patrol car, please.'

He was not having a good day with her, it seemed. After she left, he apologised again.

'Tassie Triangle? Where do they get

these new recruits? As for you, Ms Ashton, please inform us if your hubby turns up.' He gave her a card. 'It's imperative that we speak to him as soon as possible. There are some serious questions we need to ask.'

He took his leave. I didn't fancy being young Jill Isherwood at that moment.

Once he left, Paula stared at me, an expression of anxiety on her face.

'Wonder what that was all about? I mean, Bazza's no angel but he's not a bad man. He's got a lot of history, things he doesn't share with me. He was in the Gulf War and I guess being in that sort of situation . . . well, it does things to any man, or woman. He explained his moodiness and secrets by claiming he was a Scorpio.'

'But?'

'His birthday is November the twenty-third. He's a Sagittarian. You'd think he'd know that.'

I pondered that for a mo. Another little thing about my brother-in-law that

didn't make sense. He'd not been a bad hubby to Paula; Lauren apparently doted on him, and vice versa. The marriage simply broke down after three years with no one to blame. No affairs, no dark discoveries about one another. They were still friends.

I decided to change the subject. 'What about that young copper? Jill? Tassie Triangle?'

Paula grinned. 'Lots of people here reckon it exists.'

I'd done my own research years ago. Missing planes and boats between Melbourne and Tassie in the Bass Strait. There were six areas of bizarre happenings around the world, the Bermuda Triangle being by far the best known.

'Do you recall once claiming that your homework had got lost in the Tassie Triangle?' Paula said.

I'd forgotten that. 'Yeah. Mrs Bevan let me off that time. Claimed it was more original than 'my dog ate my essay, Miss'. Dad wasn't happy, though. He never liked me.'

Paula touched my shoulder. I winced.

'Sorry. I think Dad does love you in his own way. He simply likes order and you weren't his idea of a dutiful daughter. When he found you were involved in that big fight with those other girls . . . I believe that's why he took that job in New South Wales; to try and change you from the rebel you'd become.'

'That worked so well, too,' I replied sarcastically. I was really bitter about that. He'd taken me from my friends, my school, my sister and the only place I'd ever known. In a way, his actions steered me into that situation last week on the bridge at Darling Harbour. I stared at the bandage, sorry for myself and angry at him.

When I'd contacted him and Mum in their London hotel, his only response on the phone had been, 'What did you expect? You chose to get involved with that sort of life. You could have done so much more.'

That's why I was here.

Paula suggested we go outside to

the office. I guessed we both needed a distraction.

Holly immediately called her over.

'Paula. There's a bloke phoning about the feature article for the Big Southern Realtor.'

It was a fortnightly glossy magazine produced for all the estate agencies in Tasmania. In addition to pages of ads promoting properties for sale, there were features on selected properties, one per agency per issue. It cost each office quite a bit to buy the issues they'd display. However they did entice would-be buyers to visit each agency, having perused the latest offerings.

'Hello. I'm Paula Ashton, manager.' The conversation was easy to follow. It seemed he was filling in for the regular reporter who visited each house then wrote up a positive blurb to accompany photos that the agency provided. I gathered he was coming tomorrow, New Year's Eve. Paula had a property she planned to take him to herself, as the lovely Yvonne had the day off. No

great loss, I thought.

Arrangements were made to meet at ten o'clock in the office. The phone call finished, Paula had a quick word with her assistant.

'How did it go with the Benson-Smythes, Yvonne? Did you sign them up?'

'Unfortunately they chose to do a sole agency with Mandeville's, Paula.'

'They what? I was certain we had them. You told them the figure we agreed? Just under nine hundred thousand?'

'Of course. They're obviously not the sort of people we want anyway. All that time we wasted on them. Doesn't matter. There'll be others. Oh, and that lady from Verona Sands decided to give us a miss as well.'

I could see the disappointment on Paula's face. It seemed she was counting on signing them both up. Finances might be worse for the office than she was letting on. I resolved then and there to use my time here to assist her in any way I could.

* ★ ★ ★

That evening, the three of us went to the Wrest Point Casino for a sumptuous buffet meal. We had other plans for New Year's Eve. Lauren loved eating at the casino and it seemed the prices were very reasonable; less than fifty dollars for two adults and a child. It was a loss-leader to entice clients for the gambling, though neither Paula nor I was bothered about that and Lauren was too young.

We didn't go to the more expensive revolving restaurant up the top of the tower. Perhaps another night. No, tonight I was looking forward to the buffet's extensive seafood spread; Tasmanian scallops and abalone were my faves.

Wrest Point used to be the only casino in Australia. It now had a lot of competition from other capital cities. Nevertheless, the setting overlooking the river, and the food, were superb.

It was still daylight when we left. The summer solstice had been a week earlier

and it would be light until after well after nine.

'If you don't mind, Sandie, I'd like to check out Bazza's house before we head home. I've got a key. It's up near the Cadbury's factory.'

Australia's quota of the world-famous chocolate had been produced there since the twenties.

'Have you been on a tour of the factory, Lauren?' I asked my niece, as we travelled through the now quiet streets of northern Hobart.

'Yes, Auntie. Dad took me last year. It was very smelly but we bought loads of yummy choccie,' Lauren replied from the back seat. 'Mum. Can I have a Cherry Ripe before bed? It's my favourite. Dad calls me his little Cherry Ripe because he reckons I'll turn into one.'

'Good try, sweetheart. But I think all that ice cream you just had for dessert will have to be enough for tonight.'

Barry's house was in the northern suburbs. Paula had found it for him. Unlike her own unit, it had a private

garden for Lauren to play in.

It was getting dark when we pulled up outside the weatherboard house. From the outside, it was clear that Barry looked after the gardens although the powder blue paintwork on the wood was showing signs of peeling. The driveway was empty. Wherever Paula's ex had disappeared to, he must have taken his car.

'What did you want, Paula?' I enquired, as we pulled up in front of next door.

'Not sure. Some sign of where he's gone and what prompted him going off like that. He loves working at that factory. I can't believe he'd jeopardise that on some impulse.'

Lauren didn't seem to notice the conversation. I guessed she was getting tired.

'Can I come in, Mum? I left some toys here. And my purple cossie.' I remembered my niece telling me her dad had a small pool in the backyard.

'Why don't we all go in? More eyes to find where Dad's wandered off to. He doesn't have some secret girlfriend,

does he, Lauren?'

'No way, Mum. He still has your picture on the wall.'

I guessed Lauren was still hoping her mum and dad would get back together. What child wouldn't? However, she seemed cool about them still being friends with their own separate lives. I'd asked her about things last night after we read some of the books I'd bought. Her reading was pretty good for her age.

When we reached the front door, Paula was about to unlock the door when I caught a gleam of light from inside.

'There's someone there,' I whispered, ushering the two of them back towards the car.

'Dad?' Lauren whispered back.

'No, kitten. Your dad would have switched the lights on. Give me the key. I'll check it out.'

'Your arm, Sandie?' said Paula, taking Lauren's hand protectively.

'Don't worry, sis. I'll be careful. I

know what I'm doing. Do you have a torch in the car? You should ring the police, too — for all the good it will do.' I suspected there wouldn't be many patrol cars around at this time of night. Those on duty would be down at the waterfront for the yacht race.

Returning to the house, flashlight in hand, I opened the door. Someone was definitely rummaging around. A thief — or was it connected with Barry's hasty departure? I pointed my torch at the carpet, strewn with papers and other objects normally secreted in drawers or on shelves.

The intruder wasn't bothered about making a mess. The telly and expensive music system hadn't been moved, so burglary seemed less likely. There was an empty photo frame on the floor, the glass scattered in pieces around it. A light flashed from the kitchen area followed by the sound of cutlery clattering onto floor tiles. At the same time I sensed the front door opening behind me. The breeze from outside felt

cool on my bare arms; however the knowledge that there were two of them in here with me made me regret coming in alone and unarmed.

'Stupid, stupid, stupid,' I said under my breath. I was surrounded. As I began to edge backwards, I felt some glass tinkle as it broke under my feet.

Damn.

The noise in the kitchen stopped. I heard footsteps coming my way so I moved quickly to the light switch I'd noticed, praying that he hadn't turned the power off before breaking in.

Light flooded the room, blinding us all for a moment just as I heard a siren. That was quick.

I lunged at the kitchen man first, wielding my flashlight. He recovered too, parrying my desperate blow. He was fast and well-trained, dressed in black with a balaclava covering his features. Deftly he kicked at my legs, causing me to lose balance. Then he lashed out with his right fist, striking my upper arm, the one that was still healing. I cried out in

pain as I collapsed.

He must have heard the siren also because he grabbed the bag he'd dropped and ran back to the kitchen, followed by the second intruder. Oddly, the second bloke wasn't wearing a mask.

'You!' I gasped.

The raven-haired guy from the plane paused, staring at me sprawled on the floor. Then he did something totally bizarre. He knelt down, examined my wound and asked if I was OK.

Stunned, I told him I was. He touched my cheek kindly then, before I could stop him, leaned over to kiss me on the lips.

'Better than I'd hoped for,' he said, before smiling then dashing off after the other guy.

I struggled to catch my breath, furious at myself. Why hadn't I protested, at least? The scent of his musk aftershave seemed to numb me for a moment. Pushing up from my prone position, I was feeling totally humiliated as two

police officers entered. I pulled my dress down over my legs. Bad enough that Mystery Man had seen me in an embar-rassing position.

I managed to point to the rear of the property.

'They went thataway . . . '

3

I was angry at myself, and mighty sore. Paula and I spent an hour explaining things to the police. They'd immediately radioed in the break-in and assault; however no trace was found of either of the men.

I assumed Balaclava Man had ditched his camouflage gear ASAP and, as for the guy from the plane, my detailed description wasn't enough to help them find him on the now darkened streets of Greater Hobart.

'What about CCTV footage from the airport yesterday?' I asked.

They stared at me as though I were a talking platypus. 'What's CCTV?'

'Video surveillance?'

'Oh, you mean a camera. They had one in the Quarantine Hall but it broke last year. Or was it in ninety-seven?'

I threw up my arms in disgust,

instantly regretting it. Tassie was the wild west of Australia all right. Talk about travelling back in time.

'Perhaps you could do an identi-sketch tomorrow at the station, Miss Ashton?'

A hint of light at the end of a very long tunnel.

'You have a police sketch artist? That's great.'

'Mrs Carruthers. She's not exactly police but she's the best portrait artist in Hobart. Does beaut cat and dog paintings, too.'

Someone switched the light in the tunnel off, then unscrewed the bulb and smashed it on the ground. The chances of finding Mystery Man went from slim to absolutely flaming impossible.

The ambulance crew turned up to give me the once-over despite my protests that I was fit as a Mallee bull. The checked the wound in my arm. Despite her reticence, Paula had a look, became pale and said nothing. They bandaged it up again with a clean dressing.

Lauren was too tired to take it all in, fortunately. It seemed the thieves had been searching for some sign of Barry's hiding place. The police were after him also, I reminded myself. Seemed like Paula's ex-hubby was becoming Mr Popular for all the wrong reasons.

The police retrieved his passport from behind a clock where Paula explained it was hidden They told her they would take it, 'just in case the thieves return.' I suspected they already had him on a watch list at the airports and where the Spirit of Tasmania ferry sailed to Melbourne.

For a quiet bloke who worked as an engineer, he sure was a bit of a riddle. I wondered again if Paula and my niece were in danger.

★ ★ ★

When we all awoke the following morn, I realised New Year's Eve was upon us. The last day of the Millennium. Everyone was nervous about the implication

of the computer Millennium Bug although no one mentioned it any more. Perhaps that was from government assurances that everything would be OK. Or, more likely, it was from the prospect that, if our world were to fall into a technological black hole, none of us ordinary Aussies could do a damn thing about it.

Paula's paper accounts would be safe although I couldn't believe Holly wasn't using computer spreadsheets or some accountancy programme.

Yvonne was off today and Paula had returned to Barry's home to make sure it was secure, plus compile a list of missing items for the police. Consequently there were no sales staff available and, although Holly was supposedly great at talking people through our listings, no one could show them around.

I thought Holly would be ideal in that role — better than my new worst friend, Yvonne, for sure.

Along with the traditional solicitors, agents in Tassie could apparently write contracts for house sales. That made

selling and buying houses pretty fast in the state, less than two months in most cases.

I was engrossed in the banking procedures, when Holly interrupted.

'Sandie. There's that bloke here from the Big Southern Realtor Magazine asking to view the property he arranged with Paula. I sent him the details and photos yesterday.'

'Hell. I forgot. I guess Paula did, too. I'll ring her. Stall him. Offer him a coffee or something.'

Paula had indeed forgotten, asking me to go with him instead as it would take too long to drive back to the office. 'Just grab the keys and property spec sheet. Holly will give you a map. It's all arranged with the owners. They're away for the day.'

I wandered over to introduce myself to the young man who was dressed casually in a red shirt with cream slacks and trainers. He had an engaging smile.

'Gareth Jones. Pleased to meet you, Sandie,' he said, extending his hand.

56

'You're Welsh?' I asked, latching onto the melodic, lilting accent.

'Born in Cardiff but I've been over here since ninety-eight. More opportunities. I'm hoping to become a reporter.'

'Sounds like a good aim. If you're finished with your coffee, we'll head off. Have to take your car, I'm afraid.'

He drained his cup and passed it back to Holly. 'Thank you. Hope you find that envelope, Holly.'

I faced Holly. 'Envelope?'

'That friendly Mr Costello brought his rent in this morning. I thought I put it in my desk drawer.' I could see the worry in her eyes.

Gareth picked up his attache case. 'Shall we go? I have a few other viewings today. Sandie, you look stunning in that dress.'

'Thank you, Gareth. I guess it matches that shirt of yours.'

He smiled as he donned his sunnies. Dark brown hair and a light brown beard struggled to cover his round face. The facial hair didn't suit him, though.

It looked more like a covering of fluff.

Despite our trip to and from the property lasting less than fifty minutes, I found myself warming to his non-stop chat. Not that I was interested in any sort of romance, though when he suggested a trip to Kingston Beach on New Year's Day, I found myself accepting. He also offered to take me for an evening meal. I was anticipating his friendly company.

'As long as I can bring my niece along in the afternoon,' I suggested. 'She loves the beach.' It was on the Derwent River and there were no waves like those at the Sydney ocean beaches. I used to go surfing in my late teenage years around Sydney but lately I'd let it slide, preferring the gym and my tennis club.

Returning to the office, I found Paula waiting.

'How did it go?'

'Fine. Nice bloke. He asked me out tomorrow arvo. Kingston Beach. And no, it's not a date; we'll have a chaperone. Lauren, if that's OK?'

'Of course.' She grinned. 'Not a date? Riigght. Whatever you say, little sister.'

'I'm off men for good. Too many complications. Too many liars, too. But I won't say no to a day out . . . and a free meal.'

I kicked myself for my last fiasco with a guy from a dating agency. Meeting his irate wife had been one of the low points of my lack-of-love life. I'd tried to explain I wasn't aware he was spoken for. She hadn't appeared convinced.

At that point, I recollected the missing envelope.

'Did Holly find the rental money?'

Paula's smile vanished. 'Yeah. A hundred dollars short. Holly can't work it out. She never left the desk. Said she must have miscounted Mr Costello's rent and offered to make it up herself.'

'A hundred dollars?'

'I told her it was OK. Still, it's made it awkward.'

* * *

A little later, Sergeant Nolan and the youthful Jill Isherwood arrived to update us on last night's break-in. They'd been informed by the attending officers, presumably because of the link to Barry.

Sergeant Mick surprised me with his opening statement. 'That bloke that was there, the one from your flight? He turned up at the station this morning. Saved us doing that identi-sketch.'

'By the cat-portrait lady,' I added. The Sergeant gave me a withering stare; however I did notice a subdued Jill break into a grin.

'Did he admit to breaking in?'

'On the contrary. He maintained he was walking by, heard a fight inside and went to investigate. He said he chased the guy that attacked you but he got away. He's no longer a Person of Interest.'

'What?' The fact that he'd kissed me when my guard was down didn't help my mixed feelings. 'The lying so-and-so. Walking by? In a cul-de-sac? I hope you locked him up?'

The sergeant suddenly became defensive.

'No, we didn't, Miss Ashton, and I resent your tone. We know what we're doing.'

'That would be a first,' I muttered under my breath, struggling to control my anger. In my mind I saw the young constable sprawled on the bridge footpath, feeling for the gun that had just been snatched from him.

'I'll remind you whom you're talking to,' he replied in a commanding voice.

Jill's eyes darted between us. Her hand was on her holster cover. That was an overreaction, totally uncalled-for. Still, it made me pause.

Paula moved in front, positioning herself in between the Sergeant and me. 'Sandie. What's gotten into you? Apologise right now.'

I was shocked. Paula was angry . . . at me?

Then I understood that I wasn't there on that bridge any longer. I shook my head.

'I'm . . . I'm so sorry, everyone.' I took a deep breath. Was I ready to do this? 'I . . . was shot in the arm last week. There was a uniformed policeman involved.' I looked at the five shocked faces watching me; Paula, Holly, Sergeant Nolan and Jill. Paula knew about the shooting, though not about the Sydney policeman's involvement in the near-disaster.

The sergeant stared for a moment, before relaxing into a less belligerent stance. He was considering my revelation.

'Last week? The siege on the walkway at Darling Harbour. That was you?'

I nodded meekly. 'He shot two others also. None seriously.' It was the first time I'd talked about it to strangers. In a way, I felt relieved.

'I can understand your reaction,' said the sergeant. 'We were briefed on the incident, of course, including the incompetence of the officer you're referring to. We're not all like that, Miss Ashton.'

I took a deep breath. 'I know that . . . logically. I'm . . . I s'pose I'm still

having issues with it; lots of nightmares. Flashbacks. My head's all over the place. That's why I'm here, trying to get things straight and decide what I need to do about my future.'

I tried to blank out that recurring terrifying image of having the pistol fired at me.

Jill came over to hug me. It wasn't what a police officer should do, however her superior said nothing. Later, we chatted quietly while the others waited patiently or went about their work. Jill gave me a card with her phone number on it.

'If you need to talk, just give me a ring. Although I might say some daft things at times, I'm a good listener.'

I appreciated her heartfelt gesture. The two police left soon afterwards.

* * *

Hours after, when things were quiet, Paula called me into her office. I guessed most people had more on their

63

minds than shopping for a new house on New Year's Eve. As for me, I was glad of a break from trying to decipher Holly's spidery handwriting.

'That was some revelation this morning. I hope it helped you in dealing with things. However, it can't have done you much good, arriving here and becoming involved in all my dramas.'

'If I can lend a hand, that's the main thing. Besides, it's better than dwelling on what happened to me. I really do need a distraction, and solving this mystery with Barry might just be the therapy I need.'

'If you're positive, Sandie?' I nodded. 'Right. I wanted to talk about last night. Are you certain you're OK? You took a nasty bump.'

'No worries,' I replied. My long-sleeved dress covered the bruising that had appeared this morning. At least the colour complemented my dress. No point in adding to Paula's worries.

'Let's discuss Bazza. Where is he and what in heaven's name is going on? I

mean, he isn't perfect. Neither am I. But I simply can't believe he's involved in something criminal . . . '

I tried to put my own inexplicable unease with Barry to one side. Their daughter was a beautiful testimony to the love he and Paula once had.

Looking through the side window of the office at the passers-by, and the tranquil vision of the Derwent glistening in the early afternoon sun, I realised how much I missed the laid-back life on Tassie and my family here. Perhaps I'd focused on my career far too much. The incident had made me doubt myself and my job.

'OK. Let's get some answers. Tell me about your Bazza. What about his history, family, friends? Anything that might give us a clue.'

Paula gazed wistfully at the photo on her desk; a younger Lauren, laughing, flanked by herself and Barry in happier times.

'He doesn't have any family. His parents passed away when he was

overseas in the Army. He was in the Gulf War, you know.'

'Operation Desert Storm? I thought we didn't have ground forces there.'

'We didn't. He was there helping defend our naval ships. A member of an anti-aircraft missile team.' She paused. 'I reckon that's why he was so moody after we married. Things must have been pretty traumatic at times. All the time I've known him, he's been a loner. He's never made any friends as such, but made mine quite welcome.'

It made sense in a way. Yet I always thought he kept things to himself because of some secret in his past. I watched some tourists snapping pics of one another outside.

'What about photos of his family — his childhood? Or let me guess. There are none.'

'How did you know? The fire that killed his parents destroyed his belongings too. So tragic.'

And convenient, I thought.

'What about this break-in at work,

then? Something must have happened then to trigger all the police interest and last night's intruders.'

'Sorry, Sandie. No idea. We haven't been that close since the divorce.'

I nodded, grasping her hands to reassure her.

'I'm sure it'll work out, Paula. Some mix-up, I imagine.'

Then I recalled a comment from the local police about taking fingerprints to eliminate employees from the theft investigation.

And there was another thing. That missing money this morning. Having recalled something that had taken place that involved Gareth, I felt sickened by the implications. My return to Tassie to escape the recent trauma was suddenly taking on its own complications. I guessed even Paradise had its demons.

'You're right, Sandie. Tomorrow's Saturday, the first day of the new Millennium. Could I suggest breaking out the wine early? Just the three of us; you, me, and Holly. Let's hope things

improve for the business and everyone here in the New Year.'

'Yeah. I'll stay on the fruit juice, though. Alcohol and my meds don't mix. Besides, you'll need a sober driver if we're going to see the fireworks.'

★ ★ ★

That evening, after a homemade meal of spag bol, we set off for the Domain. It was on the northern outskirts of Hobart city with a magnificent view over the river and Tasman Bridge. Despite the warm day heralding the beginning of summer, Hobart evenings and nights could still be chilly.

There was a wonderful, relaxed party atmosphere with a few snack vans and play areas for the many children. We all had coats on plus rugs for the grass and our legs. The lateness of dusk arriving added to the peaceful ambience.

Someone had set up a Tannoy system playing music while we watched the skies transform through shades of gold

and tangerine to reds and spectacular violets. The full moon had been a week earlier.

Down below we could see the lights of the eastern shore across the river and miniscule cars weaving through the streets or across the bridge. Lauren was struggling to stay awake, even with the undercurrent of excitement. At long last the countdown began as hundreds of voices joined in the chant, erupting into a deafening 'Happy New Year!' as the fireworks announced the first day of the year 2000. We stood and danced, hugged, kissed or simply shook hands with family and total strangers. It was magical.

'Lauren. Look at the fireworks,' Paula said, pointing. Cascades of colour exploded in the skies above us for almost fifteen minutes. We knew it wasn't on the scale of Sydney's world-famous harbourside spectacular, yet that didn't matter. It was ours. It was for the visitors and populace of Hobart town, and the cheers and cries

of joy were a memorable reminder of that.

I'd almost forgotten about the drama of the last few days. Unexpectedly, I noticed a familiar face in the crowd, as we ambled back to the car park.

'Paula! It's him. The bloke from the plane.' I began to sprint to where he was sitting casually on a bench. He hadn't noticed me.

'Sandie. Wait!' Paula yelled. Through the subdued voices of the crowd, Paula's loud plea seemed to alert him. He gathered his belongings and, spying me running down the grassy slope, disappeared quickly into the dense crowd.

I'd lost him.

Panting, I collapsed onto the bench where he'd been sitting. Despite the breeze, that damned aftershave of his brought back memories of that kiss. Had he been watching us from afar? Had he been watching *me*? Why did I always pick the wrong sort of men to get mixed up with? I was so frustrated that I almost didn't notice the paper

lying on the dew-kissed grass.

I picked it up. It was a document stating there was a positive fingerprint match for Christopher Davidson.

'Chris Davidson. Who's that?' I asked myself before flipping the page over.

There was a coloured passport photo of a man with the stranger's name printed underneath. Only he wasn't a stranger at all.

'Hello, Mr Chris Davidson,' I said aloud. 'Long time no see.'

4

I didn't say anything to Paula as we drove home to her unit. Despite wanting to share this startling discovery with my sister, I was aware of a very sleepy Lauren. It had been a memorable night and there was no way I wanted to spoil that.

Once changed and tucked up in bed, Lauren was asleep within seconds. Paula and I walked back to the living area.

'Forget the medication, Paula. I need a drink. Got any cider?'

'Don't tell me you're still a cider drinker.' She opened the fridge, taking out some cab sav for herself and a can of Mercury for me.

'Normally not. But there's something about being in 'the Apple Isle' that makes me feel a little patriotic. Don't bother with a glass, thanks.'

She poured a small glass of wine for herself and we walked through to the comfy lounge area.

'I found something that the bloke from the plane left behind.up at the Domain. I reckon he's been watching us.'

'Watching us? Why?'

'No idea. But what he left . . . Have a look.'

I took a large gulp of the cider. Paula's eyes and mouth opened in shock.

'But that's . . .'

'Yeah. Your ex. Seems Barry has more history than you thought.'

It appeared that Barry Denvers was also Chris Davidson. I guessed that simple revelation had only recently become public knowledge to those searching for him. Was this the reason for his disappearance — and was it related to the break-in, the police interest and Mystery Man being around? Quite possibly. Yet what had precipitated all this attention?

'Paula. The police investigated that break-in where Barry worked. And they

73

took fingerprints?'

'You don't think . . . ?' She paused while I took another drink. 'Actually, that makes sense. Something showed up about the fingerprints. No wonder Bazza seemed a little edgy the last time I saw him. I put it down to the theft at work over Christmas but maybe he suspected his identity deception might come to light. Although, if this Chris bloke assumed Bazza's name, what happened to his Chris persona? You can't simply disappear, can you?'

I knew better. It would have made more sense to swap identities.

'You have access to the internet, don't you? Let's try putting their names in and do a search.'

'I'll have to connect via the modem thingy. But you say there might be personal information about people on there?'

Paula didn't seem to have much idea about the possibilities of using the internet, especially for her business. I knew that Holly had instigated web

pages for Paula's Real Estate agency; however they were pretty basic. It was something I wanted to advise my sister about. It was time to make technology work for her business.

'Let's just check it out,' I prompted her. We went over to boot up the computer. It seemed to take ages. Then she dialled up the internet and those irritating electronic sounds started. It was well after one-thirty in the morning by then. Nevertheless, I had a feeling that some further answers might be there.

Finally we had access to Lycos.

'Type in Barry's name,' I asked Paula. She began typing away slowly with one finger.

'Let me,' I suggested impatiently.

'You can touch type?' Paula asked.

'I can do lots of things. I'm not the clumsy little girl I once was, big sis.'

Some entries came up, but most were for John Denver. Stupid search engine.

'OK. No good.' Paula sounded frustrated. 'Try Christopher Davidson.

Wait. Put in Staff Sergeant. That's the rank on this photo.'

I typed away and pressed search. 'Looks like something here.'

'Hurry up, Sandie.'

I quickly read the simple entry to Paula. There were no photos. '*Staff Sergeant Christopher Davidson was killed January 14th 1991, in an accidental explosion of ordnance while serving with the Royal Australian Corps of Military Police.* Well, that's one way to wipe out your own life, then assume the ID of the real bloke who died. If he'd had MP training I've no doubt that Chris/Barry could change records, photos plus some fingerprint records too. There wasn't much in the way of computer records back then.'

Paula went pale, almost dropping her glass.

'You don't think he actually killed the real Bazza? That's so horrible.'

'I think he probably saw an opportunity and took it. It does seem that he was into something dodgy back then

76

and it's caught up with him again. Otherwise why disappear, and why are the police and baddies so keen to track him down?'

Paula and I were both quite drunk when we eventually crawled into our respective beds that morning. It was not a great start to the year 2000.

★ ★ ★

New Year's Day brought forth a decision to focus on having an enjoyable day out with Lauren. Paula would join us in the morning and Gareth, with the fuzzy face, in the afternoon.

I wasn't one for resolutions yet, with all that had happened lately, I was considering that maybe it was time to get serious about my love life. Gareth did present possibilities; I hoped I was wrong about my suspicions. I had no proof, so I was willing to give him the benefit of my doubt. Even so, Foxx Mulder's *X-Files* motto about trust was still in my mind.

I'd seen the nasty side of life in the seedier suburbs of Sydney. Even here in my sisterly retreat, it seemed trouble was slithering after me.

★ ★ ★

Constitution Docks were the first literal port of call. I'd been down at Sydney Harbour along with thousands of others last Boxing Day. Seventy-nine yachts had started out, with the fastest arriving at Hobart less than two days later. It was the first time I'd been there at the start and at the finish. True, January the first was a few days after the Maxis came in, but with most of the yachts having arrived, there was a carnival atmosphere all around the picturesque waterfront.

The weather was sunny and a little brisk as we wandered around soaking up the sights. Eventually, I noticed the two passengers on my plane chatting to a couple of guys.

'G'day,' I said, going over. By the time. I'd arrived, the men had left,

merging into the crowds. 'Bill and Val, isn't it? How's the holiday going?'

'Lovely. Bill and I are having a really nice time, thanks,' Val replied with a toothy smile.

Paula and Lauren arrived behind me. I introduced everyone.

'Last day in Tassie?' I asked them, recalling their desire to see everything in three days.

'Actually, we've decided to stay on. It's a nice, nice place, especially Hobart,' Val explained, taking charge of the conversation. 'Bill and I were considering buying an investment property down here. Maybe use it for the occasional break from the rat-race.'

'Oh! In that case my sister might be able to help. She's in Real Estate.'

'Oh, that's nice. If you have a business card we'll look you up. Not today of course. Everywhere seems to be closed apart from that Taste of Tasmania Festival. How about tomorrow?'

'Sorry,' Paula said. 'Tasmania doesn't open on Sundays. It's a government

thing. There's talk of change but we're not like the other capitals.'

'In any case, we will catch up. We'll let you get off then, you and your nice daughter. So beautiful. Just like her mummy. Nice to meet you all.'

As they ambled off, Paula whispered, 'He doesn't say much. As for her, she seems really . . . 'nice'.' We giggled. It wasn't meant nastily but it did seem to be the only word Val knew.

*   *   *

As it was Saturday, we all headed off to the Salamanca Market. It was packed with shoppers. We took our time, with Lauren choosing to spend some of her pocket money on a Vanessa Amorosi pencil case for her new school year that began in a month. I treated myself to a pastel green T-shirt with a photo of a snarling Tasmanian devil on the front. It summed me up in a lot of ways; *looks a bit cuddly but watch out for the bite.*

I decided I'd wear it and my emerald

bikini when we went to Kingston that arvo. The arm bandage would have to spoil the ensemble, though. So much for my all-over tan. To be truthful it wasn't that dark, these days. All that talk of skin cancer from the harsh Aussie sun had certainly changed attitudes since we were kids. Nowadays, I slapped on a high factor sun block and made sure I wore a broad brimmed hat, plus proper sunnies.

Drifting around the market, I also treated myself to a locally made handbag. Tassie craftspeople were highly respected.

I kept a wary look out for Mr Tall, Dark and Downright Sneaky. There was no sign of him.

★ ★ ★

We went back to Paula's unit for lunch before Gareth collected us at two o'clock in his silver Commodore. He was right on time, wearing the same shirt as yesterday but with board shorts and thongs on his feet. He'd made an attempt to trim the sparse fur on his face, shaping

it into something that almost looked masculine.

The thing that struck me right away was an odour that assaulted my sensitive nose. It seemed he'd been attacked by After-Shave Man wielding a litre bottle of Eau de Dollar Shop Number Five.

On the drive, I ensured that the windows were down and the blower on full. Even so . . .

Lauren took to him right away. I had to admit, he had a cheeky way, engaging her in silly jokes and conversations all the time as we drove up the Southern Outlet that led to Kingston — but I was definitely having second thoughts about him. Something wasn't quite right.

Unlike most Sydney beaches, Kingston was narrow. However, it was packed full of sunbathers.

Gareth had all the gear; mats, an umbrella, even a bucket and spade. They were worn, as if they'd been played with. I wouldn't pick Gareth as a castle building sort of bloke.

The bucket was in a sandcastle shape, perfect for moulding the damp white sand on the beach. Simply having Lauren there made my afternoon so much brighter and more fun. It was like a family day out; I was taken back to happier times on this same beach with Mum, Dad and Paula.

'Who wants an ice cream?' Gareth asked, immediately putting his own hand in the air. Lauren and I followed suit, enthusiastically. It had been a beaut time for us all, I thought. Gareth seemed to have boundless energy as he and Lauren played ball on the sand, while I lay back on my towel, reading a few pages of the latest Jilly Cooper.

'OK, I'll get them,' Gareth said, fishing out his wallet from his boardies. While he went across to the local milk-bar, Lauren and I nipped into the gentle waves for a quick cool off. Gareth had previously confessed to being a non-swimmer, coming as he did from a colder climate than ours.

We were busy splashing one another

when I noticed Gareth had returned empty-handed and was rummaging through my handbag. Good thing I'd kept my suspicious nature on stand-by.

When he came back with three double cones, I asked him about it.

He smiled in between licks of the rapidly melting ice cream.

'Sorry, Sandie. What it is, is when I got over there, I realised I didn't have enough money, so I borrowed five dollars from you. I decided you wouldn't mind.'

'No, of course I wouldn't mind. It's just I would have liked to be asked. A lady's handbag is private. You wouldn't like me to go through your wallet without permission, would you?' I gave him an inquiring glance with the biggest false smile.

That caught him out. He stopped slurping and the melting vanilla began to run over his fingers. Had I noticed the ten-dollar notes he had in his bill-fold or was I being genuinely upset at a relative stranger snooping in my possessions? I decided then and there that Gareth Jones

was not the man I'd anticipated he'd be. So much for my New Year's resolution about love.

That put a slight dampener on the afternoon from my viewpoint. I tried not to show it as Lauren demolished her own ice cream in between telling jokes, but I decided to put my new green Tassie devil T-shirt back on. I wasn't comfortable with being so exposed to Gareth's surreptitious glances at my less-than-spectacular chest any longer.

When he disappeared to the gents a little later, I checked my bag. There was five dollars missing. Only five dollars. Then I noticed him walking towards us, appearing very worried. Unexpectedly, Mystery Man was guiding him by the upper arm. By comparison, Gareth was much less muscular.

'What the hell is going on?' I demanded. The taller man was wearing a casual checked shirt and shorts, again freshly purchased and un-ironed. He also wasn't quite the man I'd originally thought. That plane trip might have muddled my

normally impeccable judgment.

There was no proof he'd been involved in the break-in at Barry's. I'd assumed he had, but there was no proof. Also, in all my years, I'd never come across such a gallant burglar. But mainly, there was that kiss . . . gentle and passionate.

I firmly believed that you can tell a lot from the way a man kisses. Not that I'd had many chances to test that theory. I'd often thought of it as a hypothesis that required more extensive testing but had never got around to it.

'My name's Adam and yes, I have been following you, Sandie. Keeping an eye on your family, really. Good thing too.' He took off his sunnies to reveal those hypnotic eyes of his. 'I believe that your date has something to admit. Tell the beautiful lady, Gareth.'

Beautiful?

Gareth was going to protest until I saw the pressure on his arm cause him to wince.

'What it is, is like I . . . I er . . . sort of borrowed one of your credit cards, Sandie.'

86

I checked my purse. I was not a happy bunny.

'You little thief!' I yelled. We were beginning to attract an audience. Reluctantly, he nodded.

The guy called Adam explained what had happened next. 'Boyo here was in the process of cloning it in his car when I caught him. Somehow he must have nicked your PIN number too.'

That was a surprise. I believed I was very protective about my security. Obviously I'd stuffed that up somewhere . . . ah, yes, it was yesterday. I'd stopped while on the way to show him the property to withdraw some cash from an ATM.

It was my turn again.

'Gareth stole money from the office too. There was a hundred dollars that disappeared.'

It made sense now. He must have pocketed it when Holly went to prepare his coffee. She must have forgotten leaving him at her desk when the missing cash came to light.

'Did he now? Perhaps you should return that too, boyo. Pretty please.'

Gareth pulled a wad of notes from one of his pockets and rapidly counted it out into my hands.

I felt sick yet relieved at the same time.

'Adam, is it? Thank you. I don't know why you're following me, though I'm guessing you're mainly after my brother-in-law. Should we contact the authorities about this slimy reprobate?'

Gareth cringed.

'Not necessary. Gareth will turn himself in to the police, first thing Monday. He'll make a full confession. That's correct, isn't it, mate?'

Gareth gulped before acquiescing.

'Monday. First thing. I'll be there.'

'You should push off now, mate. Consider your date with these two lovely ladies well and truly finished. And you can cancel that meal and hotel room you booked for tonight, as well.'

Gareth stared at Adam's stern features, clearly amazed that his plans were common knowledge.

As for me, I was lost for words. How could I have misjudged this man? Gareth sensed my suppressed fury and left quickly, after gathering up his gear. Noticing he'd forgotten a plastic ball, I picked it up and threw it after him, just missing. his bobbing head.

'Calm down, Sandie. You're better off without him.' Adam put his hand gently on my shoulder.

'You've got that right, sport. 'Spose I owe you, big time.' Somehow his closeness elicited a far different reaction to my jumpiness on the plane.

In a way it was that elusive closeness I'd been searching for all my life. I'd never admitted it to myself before, I realised with a jolt. Not that I ever wanted someone to dominate me, like Dad did Mum, However over the years, fighting the male-dominated place where I worked, it would have been reassuring to have someone to support me . . . someone to watch over me, too.

There was one big problem with Gareth's departure, though. Lauren and

I were stuck here.

Adam put my mind at ease.

'Don't worry. I'll give you girls a lift home. My rental's parked down the road a bit. I'll go get it. Meet you over the road near the milk-bar. One other thing, Sandie. It's time you and I had a chat. Some unfinished business.'

Adam headed off at a jog. Although he was the wrong side of thirty he appeared fit enough, especially in those shorts.

Lauren had been very quiet, trying to make sense of the past few minutes.

'Auntie? Is Gareth a bad man? He was very kind to me. I liked him.'

I knelt on the sand to hold her in front of me. It was time for one of those difficult life lessons . . . for Lauren as well as for Sandie Ashton.

'Sadly not all people are what they seem to be. Gareth stole from me — and your mum.'

She paused. 'And that other man . . . Adam. Is he bad too? He does look a bit scary.'

'No, sweetheart. I thought he was

and I was wrong. I believe that Adam is a good man.'

We gathered our towels and beach bags to walk over the road using the zebra crossing. As we reached the other side, there was the deafening roar of a high-powered car turning the corner. It was travelling far too quickly in this built-up area between the shops and beach.

A young boy about Lauren's age dashed past us onto the crossing. It was a slow-motion nightmare in the making. The hoons in the Valiant Charger couldn't possibly stop in time.

Dropping my bag, I released Lauren's hand as I reached out to grab the child's arm. Unfortunately I was wrong-footed and couldn't jump back to safety in time. I braced myself for impact, holding the boy close to my chest to protect him when the car struck my back.

The last thing I heard over the roar of the turbo-charged engine was Lauren's shrill voice.

'Auntie Sandie . . . '

5

Suddenly I felt an arm encircle both of us, yanking us out of harm's way. We crashed to the road, our fall being cushioned by someone ... It was Adam.

The car accelerated past scant centimetres from us. The idiots hadn't even seen the boy. He began to cry as his ice cream had dropped to the road and was now splattered everywhere by the car tyres.

We staggered to our feet, helped by concerned onlookers. Adam's new clothes were ripped and dirtied by the impact with the Tarmac. There were cuts and scratches on him as well.

I examined both the boy and me. Just shaken up. Lauren ran to our side, crying. She hugged me in relief.

Adam grimaced. 'I can't leave you alone for a minute, can I, Sandie?'

I gave him a wan smile, unable to speak because of the shock. The adrenalin was pumping through my body. I felt so cold. Protectively, I put my arms around Lauren telling her that everything was all right.

'You. Blondie. What are you doing to my son?' an indignant woman screamed.

I didn't need this.

'Saving his life,' I replied, angrily.

At that point the vocal mother noticed the splattered ice cream and the roar of the departing car. Spectators flocked round us, praising our actions. A very subdued mother apologised profusely before giving me a heartfelt hug.

I gritted my teeth. At this rate the bloody bullet wound would never get a chance to heal up.

When we finally managed to leave the crowd, Lauren squeezed my hand. She'd stopped crying.

'You're a hero, Auntie Sandie.'

I turned to Adam. 'We both are. I thought I was a goner. If you hadn't been there . . . '

I began to shake. My life was a mess, and coming back to Tassie wasn't going well.

Lauren thought I was a hero. Unfortunately I didn't feel like one. I wondered what she'd say if she knew what really happened that previous week. Hero or coward; it was a fine line separating the two.

★ ★ ★

By mutual consent, we decided to leave the drive back to Paula's for a while. Adam was hurt more seriously than he wanted to admit. The milk-bar owner invited us inside, having seen the near-fatal disaster out of his shop window.

His wife took Adam through the back, insisting that she clean and dress his wounds. He didn't want an ambulance called.

Lauren and I sat at a booth in a corner. The owner kept well-meaning witnesses away, informing us we could

order whatever we wanted, on the house. I decided I needed a tea. Lots of sugar was good for shock, apparently. And, right-now, I wasn't that concerned about watching the kilos.

'What would you like, Lauren? More ice cream?'

I could see what the shrinks meant about children being resilient. She was smiling and joking again. Maybe it was her way of coping, concentrating on the here and now.

She made one of those pensive faces, considering the suggestion.

'No. I have to be careful about my teeth, Mum says. Could I have a hamburger and chippies? And some beetroot on the hamburger, please? I love beetroot but I have to make sure I don't spill it 'cause it makes a dirty mark.'

'Of course, I said, nodding to the owner gratefully. And one for me also, if that's OK.'

The gentleman smiled broadly.

'That was the bravest thing I seen in me life, lady. Some food and drink?

Least we can do.'

The special meal out tonight with Gareth wasn't going to happen, so why not take advantage of his generous offer?

Adam returned and joined in the request for some totally unhealthy junk food. He'd scrubbed up and the few dressings were unobtrusive.

He began apologetically.

'Listen, Sandie. About that kiss the other night . . . '

Big-ears Lauren was first to speak.

'You kissed Aunt Sandie? Wow.'

I put a finger my lips. 'And don't tell anyone, especially your mum.' I linked my finger with hers. 'Pinkie promise.'

'Pinkie promise. I'll be quiet now . . . but may I have a strawberry milkshake, too?' She gave a cheeky grin. Talk about a born negotiator. The owner nodded and headed to the counter.

'Think nothing of that kiss, Mr . . . ?'

'Adam Powell. I've been searching for your brother-in-law and was keeping an eye on his house when you turned

up the other night. It was me who rang the police to come when I realised you were in danger. I'd been intending to follow the bloke who broke in but you blundering in with those lovely feet of yours spoilt those chances.'

'Excuse me? Blundering?' I asked, tongue-in-cheek. Talk about a classic back-handed compliment! Realistically, he was correct though no way was I going to admit that . . . not right now.

'Blundering, Miss Ashton.' He wasn't backing down. It was a stand-off. Lauren was watching the exchange between slurps.

'Exactly who are you, Mr Powell?'

'Can't tell you that, I'm afraid. However Sergeant Nolan is aware of my status otherwise he wouldn't have let me go so easily when I visited the police station. I believe he advised you that I'm not a person of interest? His words, not mine. That should reassure you a little.'

It did.

Adam continued. 'Suffice to say a number of people are after Barry. I'm

just one of them. But I will promise that neither you nor Barry's family have anything to fear from me.'

Our meals arrived and the owner waved away our thanks.

'OK,' I said to Adam. 'You have secrets and I accept you're not the evil criminal I thought you were. But I still don't totally trust you.'

'As it should be, Miss Ashton. Could I suggest, we suspend our concerns for today and enjoy our first meal together?'

'First? That's very presumptuous, Mr Powell. I hope you're not considering another kiss too.'

He grinned but said nothing. My guardian angel was full of secrets, it seemed.

* * *

True to his word, Adam returned us to Paula's. There was no goodbye kiss before he drove off.

That evening I settled down with Paula and Lauren to watch some telly.

Between the two of us, my sister was informed about the day's events. I didn't go into too many details though, especially about Adam.

Lauren had had an exhausting day and would be holidaying at her great-grandparents for a while starting tomorrow. Gran and Mum were both only teenagers when they had fallen pregnant, so Gran was young enough not to be overwhelmed by her great granddaughter's energy whenever she stayed on the farm.

It was dark outside when I heard a noise. Someone was moving around the communal gardens outside Paula's unit. Instantly I was on alert again. I doubted it was Adam.

'Should I phone the cops?' asked Paula. He — presumably he — was moving around outside the windows, cautiously until he tripped over something. He exclaimed a few choice words. So much for a low profile.

'I've already seen more uniforms in the past few days than I want. I'll go

and check myself first. Could be nothing. A possum, perhaps?'

I was still uncomfortable with uniformed officers for some bizarre reason. As Sergeant Nolan had said, they weren't all the same.

'Yeah, right. A possum who knows more swear words than a Melbourne brickie?' Paula folded her arms defiantly, questioning my admittedly stupid statement. I gave a shrug.

'Where's that torch?'

Paula produced the one she had in the car the other evening. It was quite battered from the scuffle but still functioned. I approached the back door, keeping the lights off. There were no curtains there and the Venetian blinds hadn't been closed. Outside, the lights of the city were quite bright; augmented by coloured Christmas lights that decorated some of the neighbouring homes.

The noise was coming closer. Finally, I saw his silhouette pass by the window over the sink.

I took a deep breath, yanking open

the door and turning on the flashlight at the same time.

There was no one there. Then I saw an envelope taped to the door frame. Inside was a photo . . . one of Barry, Paula and Lauren. A note was scribbled on the back. *Tell us where your husband is or we come after you.*

Paula told me it was from Barry's house. She was frightened. It appeared that whoever had broken into Barry's house was leaving some sort of threatening message — *we're aware of where you live too.* Things were going from bad to worse.

★ ★ ★

On Sunday morning after brekkie, I decided to phone Constable Jill to ask a favour.

I thought again about the previous night's drama. Evenings with strange men prowling around was becoming far too common since I'd arrived in Tasmania. It was like a telly show where

101

the writer had run out of ideas.

I told Jill about the situation, asking her if she knew who this Adam was and what he was doing here. She was cagy in her reply, reiterating that he wasn't 'a person of interest'.

'I'll tell you what I think, Jill. I reckon he's someone high up in law enforcement from interstate.'

There was a pause after which Jill explained she had to go. As she rang off, she paid me a compliment. 'You'd make a fantastic detective, Sandie. Better even than Sherlock Holmes.'

It must have been the way Jill's voice betrayed a hint of hero-worship that made me ask.

'You do know that Sherlock Holmes wasn't an actual person, don't you, Jill?'

'Oh,' was her simple answer. 'But that Dr Watson, he was real. Otherwise he couldn't have told us about all those exciting adventures, could he?'

★ ★ ★

It took a while to get Lauren's suitcases packed for her stay with my grand-parents down at Huonville. She wanted to take everything, 'just in case I need it'. Eventually, we were on our way. We left Hobart behind, slumbering in its usual Sunday torpor.

Having reached the flat part of the valley just past the Mountain River turn-off, Paula broached the subject of her ex. I checked on Laura. She was listening to her music on headphones.

'Should we tell Gran and Grandad?'

I was quick to respond.

'Yes. They might have some idea about his hidey-hole. Didn't you tell me about his weekend trips down the Huon for fishing and hunting?'

There was a sad tendency among Tasmanian men; partially due to the vast wilderness and lack of people. Gran once summed it up. 'Men around here have a motto; if it moves, shoot it, if it doesn't, cut it down.' The logging of trees in the forests was big business. Even on Sunday we'd already passed

three long lorries carrying tree trunks as tall as a two-storey house. The trucks were called B-doubles and, while they were common around here, you'd never see them on the crowded streets of Sydney.

'Makes sense.' Jill was weighing up the situation. Barry needed to be found by us first in order to give some answers as to why he was Tasmania's Most Wanted. 'If anyone knows the Huon, they would. It's a bloody big place, though. Lots of spots to be without anyone suspecting you're living there.'

We were both familiar with the Huon from our own childhood stays on our grandparents' property off the Glen Huon Road just outside Huonville. The local council covered over three thousand square kilometres, and stretched more than a hundred k from Mountain River down to Cockle Creek. For all that, there were fewer than fifteen thousand people living there.

'Gran's looking forward to seeing you. Nothing like a good old face-to-face

chin-wag, she said.'

I laughed. 'Ear-bashing is more like it. Reckon going to see Gran is a bit like a chook wandering around to a barbie and asking 'What's for dinner?' But it will be great to be with them again.'

'You'll have a lot of explaining to do about your life decisions. Gran doesn't mince words.' She patted my hand 'Rather you than me, Sandie. Rather you than me.'

★   ★   ★

Belvoir House had been a part of our family for generations, built before Tasmania became part of Australia in 1901. The original weatherboard property with its handmade nails had been extended over the years until it was now a sprawling homestead with eight hectares of gardens and trees.

We noticed Gran's new 'toy' as we drove through the front gates. She was mowing the grass with her blue and orange tractor. Disengaging the cutters,

she trundled alongside Paula's car up to the house itself. We made our way over to admire the impressive vehicle and say hello properly. Grandad came outside too.

'Sounds like you lot have been having a typically Ashton few weeks of drama.' Gran had never approved of our father and, these days, it was something she and I had in common.

'Come inside for a cuppa and a bite to eat.'

'Gran. It's only ten o'clock,' I protested.

'Been up since five, girlie. Time for some fuel for this old girl's tummy. You can join in or watch me eat my waffles. Your choice.'

Waffles? No one argued after that. Grandad had everything prepared for one of those sumptuous brunches that I'd almost forgotten.

The following hours were a nostalgic trip back to those times before Mum and Dad decided we'd be better off up in Sydney. I was angry that my

grandparents had virtually been cut out of my life, and they had felt the loss too.

I'd sorted my life out in Sydney just as I would have in Tassie. My rebellious phase with school was simply a phase. My dad hadn't saved me from a life of being an awkward madam. I had.

Brunch seemed to flow effortlessly into lunch. For a while, Lauren played with the cats and kittens that were always a feature of Belvoir House. Then Gran suggested a walk. Grandad stayed in his domain, the kitchen, while the rest of us did a tour of the gardens, pond and rivulet where platypuses once lived.

We admired Gran's green-thumbed handiwork. There were lilac and white agapanthus everywhere along the pathways, apples and Greengage plums nestled between the blackwoods and wattles with three huge mulberry trees providing welcome shade in the front garden.

Lauren fed the ducks as we relaxed on the wooden benches near the

crumbling wharf from which we used to swim. A kookaburra laughed from the trees up above.

We asked Gran about Barry's whereabouts. She couldn't help. In retrospect, Paula realised how secretive he was about his weekends away.

'He could have been anywhere, though I do recall some receipts for meals from Southport. I think it was Sam's Saloon. It was years ago.'

'Time to head back for lunch. His Excellency said one o'clock and doesn't like us peasants to be late. Don't say anything but he's worried about some health issues he's been having. He's seeing the doc next week.'

Fifteen minutes later, we were washed and ready for lunch.

'It's cottage pie, everyone,' Grandad proclaimed, setting it out on the huge sassafras dining table. Then he playfully nudged Lauren. 'Do you remember the difference between a cottage pie and a shepherd's pie, my little princess?'

She grinned and tossed her pony tail

over her shoulder. 'Sure Grandad. I remember. One's made from cottages and the other one has shepherds inside.' We laughed. Then she picked up a bottle of tomato sauce. 'And my cottage pie is going to have a big, red door.'

* * *

After our meal, Paula and Lauren helped Grandad clear up. Gran bent down next to my chair to whisper in my ear. 'Sandie. You and me. Outside, now. We need to talk.'

I swallowed. 'Whereabouts, Gran?'

'You forgotten, girlie? Where we always go.'

I made my way outside the original wing of the homestead to the shade of a huge magnolia tree where two cushions rested on the garden chairs. Gran joined me within minutes.

She offered me a Passiona, my favourite carbonated drink before opening one herself.

'I felt terrible when I heard you'd

been shot. How is your arm?'

'Healing.'

She unwrapped the bandages carefully. I recalled she'd seen her share of bullet wounds as a combat nurse in the Vietnam War.

'When did this happen exactly? . . . ' I told her. 'To me it looks inflamed, and that bruising isn't right. It should be healed more than it is. You haven't knocked it, have you?'

'A scuffle with an intruder at Barry's home. Oh, and saving some kid from being run over yesterday. Nothing to speak of. Should I see a doctor to check it?'

'Sooner rather than later, young lady.' She re-did the dressing and I thought no more of it.

'And you. The inside you? Guess that's why you're here. Having second thoughts about your way of life?'

I nodded.

'At least you haven't made a fool of yourself over men like your mother and sister. Something to be grateful for.'

'Well actually . . . ' I began, before telling her about my near miss with Gareth as well as the strange guy on the plane. I didn't mention that kiss though.

'You realise I can't tell you what you should do as far as your future goes. Tried that with your mother and look where that got me. She took you away from me and Paula. Hardly rings me at all. The only thing I reckon you should do is get yourself a cat.'

'A cat?' So much for expecting some sage advice from my dearest grand-mother.

'A reason to come home after work. Someone to talk to who don't answer you back. And if you have a mouse plague like we had here last year, a cat's a damn sight better than a useless man.'

I understood that she didn't include Grandad in that category; however she was dead right about some guys. Me, I was reserving judgment about Adam. He was certainly good-looking and engaging but was that enough?

As for catching mice, I reckoned Gran's cat suggestion was a better bet for sure.

'Men!' I said raising my can.

'Amen to that, Sandie.' Gran did the same with her drink.

We remained there, discussing everything and nothing for hours, finally returning to the gallery kitchen where the others were playing a game of Monopoly. A thunderous noise began in the ceiling at one end, moving over our heads and stopping at the other end of the long room. Then it began again, moving in the opposite direction. All the cats were watching the ceiling; however the people had obviously become used to it.

'Possums. It's their playtime,' Grandad explained.

'They're living inside your roof?' was my incredulous question. It sounded like a freight train was up there.

'A family. We've tried to close up the gaps when they're outside eating at night but they're clever little beggars. They prise the roof holes open again with

their paws. Even tried to drive them out by putting a radio up there playing music. They hate noise.'

'And?'

'They turned it off. Don't ask me how but I swear they did it.'

I nodded. The nocturnal marsupials were intelligent and about the size of a medium-sized dog. Turning a radio off? I could believe it.

* * *

It had been a wonderful day. Paula and I kissed Lauren goodbye before driving back to Hobart. Once back at Paula's, I decided to phone Sam's Southport Saloon to find out if they might be aware of Barry or his location. I'd kept a wary eye out for his pursuers on our drive to Huonville and back. Luckily there hadn't been any sign of them.

The phone rang out for a few seconds, then was answered by someone whose voice reminded me of a parrot's screech.

113

'G'day. Sam's Saloon. What you want?'

'Hi. Wonder if you can help me. Have you heard of a bloke called Barry Denvers visiting or living in the vicinity?'

'Don't you mean John Denver? Heard of him. Didn't realise he lived around here though. Thought he was a Yank or something.'

It was going to be one of those conversations that I was certain would give me a headache. 'No. Not John Denver. His first name is Barry.' Then I had a thought. 'Maybe he's going by the name of Chris Davidson?'

'Naw, darling. Don't recognise that name either. Do know Aihara Ryushi, if that's any help. Bit of a drongo and a dole bludger to boot. You want to speak to him? He's at the other end of the bar.'

I gave a silent sigh.

'No thanks, Miss. Sorry to bother you.'

She didn't seem to hear me because

114

she hollered at the top of her voice. 'Aihara? Some nosy mainland sheila wants to talk — '

I quickly hung up, wondering if her voice had deafened me for life. So much for that idea.

And fancy her calling me a mainlander! Do I really sound that different?

6

We both relaxed with a drink. The telly was switched on low. Tonight was our first chance to catch up properly. Paula had rung to check on Lauren. We were both concerned about her well-being after the last few days.

'Lauren was over the moon that she helped Grandad bake some pumpkin scones after we left. Seems to be enjoying being there.'

'That's good. I imagine Gran and Grandad are loving it too. She doesn't seem to be as much of a trouble-maker as I used to be.' I shuddered when I recalled some of the naughty things I'd done at Lauren's age. It was time to change the subject.

'Paula. Could you tell me more about Barry? It may give us some clue as to where he is.'

Paula turned to me, a spark of

annoyance appeared on her normally pleasant features.

'About that, little sis. Quite frankly, I honestly don't care much about Bazza's present predicament. We were married for four years but we were really together as a couple for less than three. Even though he's Lauren's father, we're not that close. I sensed he had a past where he did things that he wasn't proud of; probably to do with his time in the Army. And the more I think about it, the more I'm not pleased that Lauren's dad is on the run from the authorities or that he chose to actually adopt the identity of another soldier. What the hell has he done?'

She touched a hanky to one eye.

'Sorry if I upset you, babe. I'm afraid I see things differently from you,' I said.

'You're concerned about Lauren and me. I understand that. But I can care for Lauren myself,' she continued.

I didn't ask 'Who will look out for you, though?' as I sensed that Paula

117

wouldn't normally be this indifferent to Barry's plight.

'You're concerned about another problem, Paula. The business?'

She stood up and slowly paced around the room before answering.

'You were always the empathic one. And yes, it is the business. We're haemorrhaging money far too much and it's not simply bad luck that Mandeville's getting all the lucrative property contracts. The trouble is, we need a computer upgrade and it costs a lot to buy the programme. I simply don't have the cash flow to do it.' She stared at her clenched hands. 'Why do you think I asked you to help out in the office, even though you clearly have your own issues to resolve?'

I moved over to hug her. 'Paula. I've seen enough of the books to have realised that already. But my accountancy knowledge is way out of date so it would be like putting a Band-Aid over a broken leg. You need a consultant to come in and set things up. I don't have

anyone local I can recommend, though if you have a person who you could use, I'd gladly pay for them to come in for a month to sort things out. Plus all the computers and software you need.'

She pulled back from me, considering my proposal. 'There is a Mainland bloke who retired here in Hobart a few months ago. He and his wife bought a house not far from Bazza's. He won't be cheap.'

'What else do I have to do with my wages? I have my unit and car and nothing else in my life at present. The hols to Thailand can wait. It's not as though I'm short of cash, sis.'

'I'll pay you back.'

'You don't need to. On the other hand, if you're suggesting that Mandeville's are deliberately sabotaging you, then we need to do some serious investigating. Otherwise, whatever we do might be for nothing.'

I hoped that my reassurances would allow Paula to have a restful sleep that night, ready to face the first working

week of the year 2000. Meanwhile, I spent a lot of my night planning and coping with my increasingly painful arm. Eventually, I chose to take one of the stronger painkillers I had been prescribed. Maybe I should visit a doctor about it after all.

★ ★ ★

Monday morning at the office was relatively quiet. There was me on the reception desk with Yvonne and Paula available to talk to prospective or existing clients. It gave me some time to do more work on the paper accounts as well as make arrangements to see the consultant guy that Paula had mentioned.

His name was Stephen Hopkins and he appeared to relish the idea of doing work again. He said he'd come to Paula's office at three that arvo. He was bringing in a new computer plus the accounts programme that I would order from a local specialist shop, based on

his recommendations. Thailand could wait.

The couple from next to me on the plane arrived for a consultation with Paula about properties available to purchase in their price range. To me, Val and Bill didn't seem that interested in what they were being shown on the computer screen in Paula's office. I couldn't quite figure it out. I had some absolutely fruity-loop idea that they might have been sent by Mandeville's to spy on our office? It seemed unlikely yet, when I first met them they were simple tourists without a clue about our state. Virtually overnight, they were supposedly keen to buy here.

There was the furtive way Bill kept glancing around every part of the office, including me at my desk. I smiled at him when he realised he'd been noticed. Like Mystery Man on the plane, he didn't look away immediately.

Or possibly I was becoming paranoid, imagining things that weren't there. Gran might be right about

getting a cat to speak to, because being all alone wasn't any fun.

★ ★ ★

Val and Bill came out from the room clutching a half-dozen property spec sheets.

'Any calls?' Paula asked me.

'Mr and Mrs Dobbs confirming your visit at four to discuss listing their house. Do you want the address?' Paula took out her Filofax.

'Shoot,' she said, without thinking. I winced. The memory of that bullet was far too raw. 'Sorry, Sandie. What is it, please?'

'Sixty-seven, Bandicoot Gardens, Taroona.' She wrote it down.

'Just taking the Eastmans round the corner to view a unit. You be all right?'

'Course I will. Bye,' I called. She waved back.

As the trio left for the viewing in Paula's car, the phone rang. It was Constable Jill Isherwood wondering if she and Sergeant Nolan could come

around to update me on my would-be lover Gareth. He'd come into the station and was very thorough in confessing to a number of thefts. Adam had certainly made an impression on the dishonest scuzzball.

'Better if I come to your station, Jill. No offence but regular visits by the police might be causing a few tongues to wag. Holly will be back at one. I'll see you around then if that's OK?'

She said it was. I'd grab a taxi there and back in time to discuss things with Stephen about the account ledgers.

When I replaced the receiver, Yvonne ambled over from doing her nails. They were now blood red, so suitable for a witch. The sound of her high heels resounded through the office and her dress revealed far more cleavage than it should.

She leered down at me.

'You're not as much fun as Holly, I have to say. At least this place feels somewhat alive when she's here. Plus you never brought me my elevenses,

like Holly does. When did you say you were going back to your dreary proper job, randy Sandie? Soon, I hope.'

It was obvious that Yvonne thought she had me summed up as some sycophantic mouse from our encounter on that first day I'd been here. It was time to put her right. Just because she was years older than me didn't give her any right to be rude, or a bossy hen at the top of some imaginary pecking order.

Time to knock this old chook off her perch.

I gave her my sweetest smile.

'I'll be around for a while, Vonny. As for preparing your drinkies, I'm sure you can wave your wand or twitch your pointy nose.'

I returned to studying my ledgers, ignoring the smouldering hatred now directed at me.

'You can't talk to me like that, you stuck-up bloody cow. I'm important around here. I'm the top saleswoman in this office after Paula.' Her voice was

loud and agitated, as well as sounding almost as screechy as that woman at Southport.

I didn't look up — or point out there were only two salespeople so she was second out of two. Instead, I lowered my voice, keeping my cool.

'Lady. In my job, I eat people far tougher than you for breakfast. The guy who shot me is lucky to be alive so, unless you wish to apologise, I suggest you crawl back to your fingernail painting and leave me alone.'

I watched her. shadow hesitate before she scurried off back to her desk, her heels rapidly clickety-clacking on the parquet floor.

I decided to celebrate my victory with a large Polly Waffle I'd bought earlier.

★ ★ ★

It wasn't far to the police station on Liverpool Street. Once I introduced myself I was taken through to an interview room. I'd seen a few of these in my

short life, Jill and Mick Nolan came in together, holding a thick document file.

'Well. What's happened?' I couldn't contain my curiosity.

The sergeant chose to answer. 'Firstly, I'd personally like to thank you and Adam for putting us on to him. He owned up to quite a few thefts of monies and goods. His solicitor tried to shut him up but he came clean once we said we were doing a property search. Even had a list of what was taken and from where. Very handy for us.'

'How many? Robberies, I mean.' I figured there were a few from the For Sale houses he'd visited to do reviews about.

'Fifteen,' answered Jill. 'We knew about some but a lot of the jewellery went missing weeks before it was noticed. We were searching his house when his wife and kids arrived home from a family trip to Perth.'

'Gareth? A wife? Wow. I didn't suspect that.'

Mick Nolan grinned. 'She said a

number of words I've not heard from a woman before when she discovered what he'd planned at the hotel Saturday night. Oh yes, she made a few threats about surgery too, the sort that didn't involve anaesthetic. Mr Jones opted to forgo bail when we told him. Said he'd be safer banged up.'

'So a good result all around, Jill?' I asked, pleased that things had worked out.

Mick Nolan closed the file. 'Constable Isherwood did an excellent job with statements and interviews of the victims. She'll need to take one from you as well, Miss Ashton. I foresee a long career ahead for our latest young member of the Tasmanian police.'

'Gee, thanks, Sarge.'

'Sergeant,' he said although not as brusquely as I would have expected. Suddenly I felt giddy and nauseous at the same time.

'You OK?' Jill asked. 'I'll fetch some water.'

'Yeah. Water. Feel a bit crook,' I tried

to joke through the pain. I gulped down a tablet with the water, gradually feeling my illness easing.

'Perhaps you should see a doctor. There's one we use nearby.'

I nodded. Gran had told me the arm didn't look right.

Jill returned after a few minutes.

'Five-forty this arvo. I've written her address down.' I took it from her gratefully, even though the terrible sensation had passed.

The sergeant asked if we could continue.

'Yes, please. I wanted to ask about Barry Denvers. Why do you want to speak to him? The fingerprints?'

Mick Nolan leaned back on the wooden chair, considering my request.

'Yes, Miss Ashton. When we took his fingerprints at the factory break-in they came back with two matches.'

I spoke up. 'Barry Denvers and Chris Davidson.'

The two police seemed surprised that I knew.

128

'And Chris is dead . . . supposedly. An accident in the Gulf War,' I said, putting all my cards on the proverbial table. I produced the paper that Adam had dropped on New Year's at the Domain.

Although Jill was about to say something, Mick silenced her with a look. 'Looks like my Constable was right about you making a great detective. Chris Davidson is wanted by police for stealing some valuable artefacts from the Middle East during the war there. The trail went cold when he 'died'. Looks like he staged his own death and assumed the identity of Barry Denvers. Here's a photo of the real Barry, taken with his parents in 1990.'

I examined it closely. There was some resemblance. Add a beard, and new Barry would pass for old Barry. Mick took it back from me.

'And the reason those men broke into Barry's house?' I enquired. Again Jill was about to speak but Mick jumped in first.

'We're not certain. Best we can come up with is either revenge from his fellow thieves or possibly he has something they want.'

My mind was racing. 'Some of the treasure? They want their cut. But how did they find out that Barry — sorry, Chris, was still alive and living in Hobart? Wait, don't tell me. They had access to police records.'

'She's dead right, Sar . . . Sergeant. That's the only explanation. A crooked copper.'

'Or support staff. Civilians would have access to restricted files too,' was my suggestion. It seemed more logical.

Barry Denvers. Theft? Possibly murder? What the hell had my ex brother-in-law done?

* * *

Back at the office, I filled Paula in about the day's events. Yvonne had already made her own complaints about me, although my only concerns were

130

for Paula and her business.

Holly was back. I realised then that Yvonne was right about one thing; I wasn't a people person. Holly had that special something about her that made clients like her instantly and, more importantly, trust her. She was a real asset.

I spent the time up to three o'clock readying the accounts as best as I could. Stephen Hopkins arrived right on time, dressed in shirt and tie just as if he was going to work in some high-rise bank or financial office building. I took to him straight away.

'Stephen. I'm Sandie. Great to have you helping out.' He was balding with a laurel wreath of grey hair and a moon-shaped face. He pushed back his thin, gold glasses onto the bridge of his nose, beaming such an engaging smile before shaking my hand warmly. Then he lifted some of the equipment that he'd collected from the computer store and followed me with a slight limp to the area I'd set up.

Holly brought the remaining cardboard boxes from Stephen's car parked outside while Yvonne watched from her own desk, clearly unsure what was happening.

After forty minutes we had the accounts programme installed. Stephen certainly knew his way around this spreadsheet and was doing his best to guide me through it also. Realising I didn't have a clue what he was on about, I explained it would be best for him simply to get on with it.

Paula came out to be properly introduced before she headed off for her four o'clock appointment. She seemed pleased and confessed that she felt a huge weight had been lifted from her shoulders.

I had my own appointment with the doc later, not before time. My fingers were aching quite a bit on my left hand. Stephen was already entering names and full details of Paula's rental clients into the impressive spreadsheets. I was very optimistic.

The time was half-past four. I expected Paula to be back soon. She'd told me she'd drive me to my doctor's appointment.

My own mobile rang, distracting me from the ongoing commentary by Stephen. It was an unknown Hobart number.

'G'day,' I answered.

'Sandie. It's Jill. I'm ringing from the station. It appears that there's a problem. Was Paula going to a house in Bandicoot Gardens?'

'Y . . . yeah,' I answered apprehensively.

'You'd better get down there quick smart. It seems she's been injured. Someone just tried to kidnap her.'

7

I was frantic. 'Kidnapped? Are you positive?' In contrast, Jill's voice was cool, calm and objective. 'No, we're not positive. Because we've already been dealing with both you and your sister regarding Barry, Sergeant Nolan and I have been assigned to this incident. The two might be related.

'We'll collect you in five minutes and drive to the scene. You may be able to assist. Believe me, Sandie. The police are taking this very seriously.'

It sounded like it too. Trying to phone Adam on the number he gave me simply rang out without answer. Therefore I made my excuses, deciding to make everyone aware of the situation and why I was leaving early. The office closed at five-thirty in any case. I trusted Stephen to work to his own pace and charge me accordingly. He'd

already agreed an hourly rate that was more than acceptable.

I dismissed ringing Gran to tell Lauren until I had more info. Waiting on the footpath, I was aware of how worked up I was.

The patrol car screeched to a halt close to me. I got in. The sergeant was driving.

As I buckled up, I heard Jill ask 'Sirens?' Mick nodded. Time was crucial.

The blues and twos started up. It was British slang for the flashing lights and two toned sirens of emergency vehicles over there and was becoming increasingly popular with Aussie police slang as well.

It was clear from the deft way that Mick steered the high powered Ford Falcon that he was a trained pursuit driver. We were at Bandicoot Gardens in moments. Two other cruisers were there already, their flashing blue and red lights indicating to all that a crime had taken place.

Another sergeant ran over, telling us

that Paula was injured but OK. She was already on her way to hospital. The old Datsun used by the would-be kidnappers had been stolen an hour before.

Apparently the Datsun had been waiting for Paula to arrive for her appointment. The occupants had attacked her, then tried to bundle her into their car. Some policeman challenged them. When he used his car to block their escape route, they panicked. In a desperate bid to avoid capture, they'd driven off across a grass verge leaving Paula sprawled across the footpath. There were two of them.

A forensic team was already taking prints and photos of some muddy footprints.

Sergeant Nolan's radio buzzed. He answered the call and announced to us all that the wanted car had been spotted heading south on the Huon Highway by a traffic camera. Patrol cars were closing in from Huonville and from Kingston, however I knew how many back roads there were on that lengthy stretch of road.

Immediately I realised that they might be going to grab Lauren too.

'Sergeant Nolan. Paula's daughter, Lauren, is staying with our grandparents at Belvoir House just on the other side of Huonville. You don't think . . . ?'

He reacted quickly, lifting his radio. 'I'll sort it, Miss Ashton.' We listened as he spoke to Huonville police, asking for undercover police to go there. I didn't want Lauren to find out about her mother's situation, at least not yet.

'Don't worry. An officer will phone ahead to your grandparents. The undercover officers will pretend to be some friends coming for an overnight visit. We won't let Lauren be in danger.'

That was a massive relief. Yet the question remained. Why try to take Paula when she clearly had no clue as to the whereabouts of Barry?

* * *

Once it was clear that there was nothing more I could do there and, with the

137

promise from Mick that I'd be updated on developments immediately, I decided to go to the hospital. The policeman who'd foiled the attempt was there too as he'd been slightly injured.

'Constable Isherwood will take you,' the Sergeant said. 'No arguments.'

On the way, Sergeant Nolan rang to update us. The stolen car had been found dumped in a township off the main highway. It was obvious they'd swapped over to another car that had already been left there. We weren't dealing with amateurs. In any case, they were checking for fingerprints or clues.

On the way, I told Jill that she didn't need to pretend with me any longer. I'd seen through her 'dumb bunny' act.

She was laid back in her response.

'Appearances can be deceiving. Men look at me and see some air-headed, skinny sheila who couldn't hurt a fly. They think I'm no threat to them so they boast about things they've done or show their real nature. And women don't see me as a threat so they trust

me with secrets that they'd never share with a man. I don't have to be a tough, no-nonsense cop when I'm surrounded by cops like that already. I'm the other one; the one you should be most afraid of.'

I began to understand how wrong I'd been about her.

'I'm an expert marksperson. I'm trained in self-defence, too.' Her statement wasn't arrogance, just a simple fact.

'Top of your class in maths, science and criminal law?' I surmised.

'Maybe? Maybe not. A girl should keep some secrets, shouldn't she?'

'Returning to your statement about being an excellent marksperson; I've a question about that, Jill. If you had to shoot a real human instead of some paper target or figure, could you do it?'

There was a lengthy pause.

'If your life and those of civilians depended on it . . . ?' I prompted.

'I . . . I honestly don't have an answer. I pray I never will be in that situation.'

It was a sobering thought; one that

we both considered.

'I'm betting that Sergeant Nolan understands who you are under your innocent façade. You're his secret weapon, aren't you? Also, most of your colleagues aren't aware of the real Jill Isherwood. That explains why you and Mick are joined at the hip.'

As I opened the car door to alight at the hospital entrance, Jill had one final bombshell to drop. Why she chose then to do it, I didn't understand.

'You and I went to the same school, Sandie. I was much younger, and you probably don't remember me at all. Nevertheless I should tell you that you're the reason I chose to be a police officer, so I owe you a lot. I've opened up more to you today than I have to almost anyone. Something else to wonder about.'

Even though I wanted to find out what she meant, Jill ignored my requests. Talk about infuriating. As I made my way into the hospital, I took another painkiller, buying some water to wash it down.

I had to stay for a while outside the Emergency Ward until the doctors had finished an initial assessment. As Paula was wheeled by on a gurney she was aware enough to wave. There were another few minutes of interminable waiting until I was given permission to enter her private room.

I rushed to her side. She was wide awake with a bandaged leg and head. There was a drip attached to her arm.

'Dextrose. To rehydrate and boost her energy,' the protective middle-aged nurse explained as though she sensed my concern.

'Is Lauren . . . ?' Paula asked.

'She's fine, Paula. Sergeant Nolan arranged protective cover for her.'

Paula seemed to relax.

'Thank the stars they didn't hurt you too badly,' I said.

She nodded. 'Have to agree with you on that point, sis.'

The nurse checked her blood pressure

with the sphygmomanometer before asking me to wait outside while they did some more tests. There was a uniformed officer there. I decided to search out the officer who'd stepped in to save Paula from being snatched. Apparently he'd already been discharged.

It was time to check on my big sister again. Strangely the female officer, who should have been on guard outside, didn't appear to be there. I walked down the corridor expecting her to be just around the corner. A nurse was approaching, with medicines on a tray.

'Excuse me. Where's the policeman assigned to room 117?' I asked quickly. I was getting a bad feeling.

'Oh, her. A plain-clothed officer dismissed her. He's in talking to Mrs Ashton right now.'

Panic was beginning to build in my chest. Things didn't feel right. There had already been an attempt to grab Paula and I was certain there were no plain-clothes officers assigned to this case as yet.

I began to sprint back towards Paula's room.

'But . . . he said he was a policeman.' I shouted back. 'Call security! Quick!'

My shoulder was aching from the exertion. I tried to hold my left arm against my side and stomach. I opened the door with a bang. My sister wasn't in the bed or anywhere in the room.

'Oh, hell. They've taken her!' I exclaimed. And I had no idea where.

8

Someone came in through the door behind me. I spun around. It was Adam.

'Where is she? I thought you were keeping an eye on us all. But they've taken her.'

Adam seemed perplexed.

'What's all the noise about?' It was Paula's voice. She came out of the en-suite bathroom, wiping her hands on a towel.

I breathed a sigh of relief. 'You're safe.' I ran up to hug her, still wary of that darn shoulder. Then I remembered the doctor's appointment. I'd missed it.

'Of course I'm safe. The Superintendent foiled the kidnapping.' Paula nodded towards Adam.

'You? You're a cop? You sent the officer outside away?'

'There was no need for her. I'm here now. And yes, I'm police.'

Two burly security men burst into

the room. Adam pulled a warrant card from his pocket.

'False alarm, guys. Sorry about that.' They left as quickly as they came.

I asked to see it also. Apparently he was Adam Powell, a Superintendent with the Australian Federal Police. The card appeared to be genuine.

'You're a Fed?' I asked, totally surprised. Adam didn't react. Obviously a man of few words.

Paula spoke up. 'Yes, Sandie. A Superintendent, no less. That's pretty important, isn't it?'

'I . . . I guess. I don't know. Superintendent is a desk job though.' I was still wary.

Adam said, 'What do I need to do to convince you then, Sandie?'

I was feeling quite woozy from the exertion but I wasn't going to show him how weak I was.

'Adam. Show her your thingy,' Paula demanded.

Both Adam and I stared at her in shock.

'I mean, that letter from the Prime Minister.'

Adam's stunning blue eyes didn't blink as he continued to stare at me.

'Somehow I don't believe your sister will believe that either. She's far too suspicious.'

Paula seemed frantic.

'How about the Kiss of Truth?'

Again we both were shocked.

'I think some of the meds might be affecting your sister, Sandie,' Adam suggested.

I had to agree. Adam's expression had changed from angry to slightly bemused. His face was still very close to mine.

There are two ways that people can react in times of stress. These past few days certainly qualified for that. Firstly you can over-think the situation, becoming depressed or even paranoid. That's what happened to me after Darling Harbour. The second option is to do something totally bonkers to release all that anxiety.

Adam chose the latter.

'This Kiss of Truth? We could try it . . . if it helps to convince you?' he said, grinning.

'So one kiss isn't enough, Mr Powell?' I blurted out without thinking. His decision to joke about the drama had drawn me in. Paula laughed.

We listened intently to Adam's response.

'Actually it was more of 'the kiss of life' . . . artificial resuscitation. No way was it a proper kiss. But now you mention it . . . '

He was doing his best to cover up my faux pas, however he was making it even worse.

Paula persisted with a slightly slurred voice. 'What about it, Sandie? The Kiss of Truth always works, you said.'

I glared at her. Drugs or no drugs, she'd pay for this humiliation.

'No, no way, absolutely not.'

Adam wasn't going to stop his playful interrogation.

'Well, at least you could explain, Sandie. About this Kiss of Truth bit.'

I realised that Paula was enjoying watching my unease with this guy. She decided to explain, determined to make me cringe even more.

'My little sister was a Wonder Woman fan. She came up with her own superheroine; Devil Damsel.' Paula put her hands to her temples appearing to concentrate on my best-forgotten past. 'Let me see. Devil Damsel was Tasmanian, naturally. While walking in the forest, she was befriended by a mystical Tasmanian devil who gave her magic powers. Instead of Wonder Woman's lasso of truth, DD had a Kiss of Truth. She could also become invisible when she was embarrassed. And she had untidy, blond hair and loved *Neighbours*.'

Mortified, I sat down on the only chair in the room. My fledgling relationship with Adam Powell was over.

Adam smiled before bursting out into one of those Santa Claus-type laughs. Paula joined in.

He forced himself to stop.

'Devil Damsel would go around kissing people to learn the truth from them? Sounds like a wish fulfilment fantasy to me. I assume it was only guys she kissed?'

I began to grin, understanding that all was not lost with him. 'Mostly. To an eleven-year-old girl, it seemed like a fab super-power to have. And I already knew that boys lied more than girls.'

I decided this silliness had gone on long enough. 'So, you really are a Fed then. No wonder I reckoned you were hiding something when I spotted you on the plane. You definitely need some training in undercover work, Mr Mystery Man.'

He brushed his black hair from his forehead, revealing a scar near the hairline and became all professional once more.

'I was watching for Barry at his house last Thursday night. I noticed the break-in and was going to follow the burglar but then the three of you turned up. As I told you yesterday, I phoned the police.

Then I entered the house after you, Sandie, ended up in that fight. I tried to catch him. I must apologise about leaving you on the floor with your dress up around your . . . '

'No need to tell the world what you saw, Mr Fed. But thanks for getting the cops there so quickly.'

I could have been badly injured by that burglar; however I realised now that Adam would have helped if it had come to that.

Adam reminded us about the serious nature of the investigation. 'I suggest we all go over to Hobart Police HQ to formulate an action plan. You two deserve to be put in the picture. It's all a matter of national security but it's my decision as to who's involved.'

I pushed myself to my feet, almost tripping on the vinyl floor. Adam caught my good arm to steady me. He was very rugged and strong.

For a moment I sensed that connection between us, however he broke into a fit of laughing again.

'Kiss of Truth? That's priceless. You are one strange lady, Sandie Ashton.'

At that moment, invisibility sounded like the absolute best power to have.

★   ★   ★

We convened in a large room within the Police Headquarters close to the city centre. Following Adam through the hallways and past security points, I came to appreciate that he'd already been here and was treated with due reverence to his rank, despite him wearing civvies.

Naturally Mick and Jill were there, talking to a senior officer they referred to as Commander. He left, as Adam completed setting up a slide projector connected to one strange portable computer I hadn't seen before.

'It's called an iBook,' Adam explained. 'Made by Apple. State of the art.'

I didn't want to show my ignorance by asking who Apple was.

We sat down with plastic plates of snacks. Finally Paula and I would find

out what the hell was going on. If there was a Federal Police Superintendent, waving around a document from our PM, giving him anything he wanted, things were serious. Adam sat with the police on one side of him and the two of us on the other. We were all able to see the large movie-type screen.

The lights dimmed as Adam reached across to press a button. His arm brushed against mine, reminding me again to see the doc pretty quickly. The sharp pain was now dull and spreading.

The screen lit up on the white and aqua machine. At the same time Barry's photo showed up on the large screen in front of us.

Adam began his presentation. 'This man was born Chris Davidson. He was supposedly killed in an explosion in Operation Desert Storm nine years ago. He was a military policeman assigned to some covert work relating to preserving valuable relics in Kuwait. He and two other soldiers were under investigation at the time of his supposed death.'

152

'What sort of investigation, Superintendent?' Mick enquired.

'Call me Adam. This is better if we drop the formality. Same goes for you two.'

'Geez. I can call you Mick, then, Sarge?' Jill said. An icy glare was his unspoken response.

'Or perhaps not,' Adam decided. 'Getting back to the investigation. It seemed Chris was a member of a smuggling gang who were intent on stealing valuable antiquities. They were forwarding the items back to Australia to a man who was the mastermind of the operation. We have his code name; Magnus. That's all the info we have on him; a made-up name. He's very secretive and seemingly has spies and connections to a number of government agencies including law enforcement. That's how he's kept one step ahead of any attempts to capture him.'

Mick interrupted. 'I thought Magnus was an urban myth.' He'd clearly heard of him, as had I — one of those

larger-than-life characters, like Ned Kelly.

'It appears that Chris stole an item so unique that he chose to keep it for himself, cutting Magnus out of the loop. Before he could be caught by his former boss, he died . . . or so we were all led to believe. Instead he settled here, as Barry Denvers, presumably keeping the antiquity for himself.'

Paula chose to become involved in the questions. That was reasonable, considering that she'd been attacked by Magnus' henchmen.

'What was so valuable, anyway? If it was Kuwait, I'm guessing gold or precious jewels?'

'No, nothing like that,' answered Adam, pressing a button on the computer. A new image flashed up.

'A knife? You're kidding, right?' Mick exclaimed.

I studied the image. 'Doesn't resemble any Arabic knife I've seen. They're usually more ornate, curved handles and such. I think the curved blade one is

154

called a jambiya?'

Adam socked us all with his next revelation.

'It's not Arabic. It's British. We believe it was taken there in the Crusades, although no idea why. However finding it is a top priority for the Australian Government. That's why I'm involved. I'll be asking you all to sign the official se — '

Paula broke in. 'I remember Bazza showing me that knife! Said he bought it for a tenner at a Trash and Treasure market in Kingston.'

I noticed Jill stand to examine the photo more closely. The Federal Officer ignored her, continuing to speculate.

'Therefore he had it back then, and presumably he still does. How long ago did he show you, Paula?'

'Years. Not long before we broke up.'

'That knife. It's Carnwennan, isn't it?' Jill interrupted, excitedly.

Adam stared at the policewoman with his mouth agape. 'How could you possibly know?'

Jill realised that she'd over-stepped her dumb-brunette facade. I saw Mick put a finger to his own lips, signalling her to be more prudent.

She regained her composure quickly. 'I read about it in a comic last week. Sherlock Holmes used it to kill The Hound of the Basketballs . . . I think?' She smiled apologetically. Adam relaxed, though he continued to eye her warily as he resumed his explanation.

'Let's simply say that it's very valuable and Australia wants it so we can return it to Great Britain. It has great historical importance.'

Paula was becoming impatient. 'What about those two thugs who tried to abduct me? Were they working for Magnus?'

'Most probably. At the hospital, you stated that one had an Italian accent?' He changed the image on the screen. It was a police full-face/side profile photo. 'This is Luigi Columbo. And you said the other one had red hair on his hand?'

Another photo; this time of a

hard-faced brute. 'Jimmy Fletcher. Everyone calls him Mad Dog. He's the hard man of the pair even though he does have a few kangaroos loose in the top paddock. The trouble with Mad Dog is that he is so unpredictable, passive one minute but easily sent off the rails.'

I decided to move the briefing on to the next bit of the puzzle. 'Paula. I cannot understand why they tried to kidnap you . . . unless you know where Barry's hiding.'

'I don't. Maybe they wanted leverage to force Barry to give himself up but I doubt that he would. We're not that close — especially now.'

Mick spoke up. 'We found the Datsun they used. The forensic boys did find something unusual; a till receipt from a shop in the Huon Valley. Some out-of-the-way place called Lon-navale.'

'I know that place,' I exclaimed. 'Run by a bloke called Bruce . . . '

What followed was a heated debate.

We were confident that we'd be able to track down the two villains who had tried to seize my sister. Paula and I knew the Huon well and if we stumbled, we had enough contacts to assist us. It was a vast area. On the other hand, the locals who lived there would be fully aware of strangers moving in.

The problem came down to how the two should be dealt with once we discovered their whereabouts. Mick had already checked the list of visitors coming to Tassie this past week and, since their names weren't there, we assumed that they were travelling under aliases.

'I reckon we send in a strike force.' That was Mick's belief for the best approach. 'We have trained officers in the Special Operations Group based in Hobart, Adam.'

'The Soggies are effective but they are part-timers, Mick. I don't want them directly involved. I understand these two. One sniff of police nearby

and they'll scarper into the forest, believe me. They're ex-army. They probably have a police radio scanner set up already. No, I want the Soggies in reserve but no closer than two clicks away. We'll use mobile phones to communicate. Despite being a Super, I'm not totally over the hill.' He grinned confidently. 'I can handle myself.'

Maybe it was bravado. Maybe he actually believed that. However I'd seen him in action. He was good, yet he wasn't as young as he used to be and I could sense his reflexes weren't up to field standard.

'You'll need a guide. I'm volunteering. I know that part of the Huon Valley probably better than any police, even the ones based in Huonville.'

I was volunteering for some dangerous work here and no one was happy about that — especially Paula.

'I can't put a civilian in danger.' Adam was equally stubborn.

'I won't be in danger. Once we identify their hideout, I'll drive you near

to there and stay in the car. You might have to walk a few hundred metres without your Zimmer frame, old man, but I believe you can handle that.'

I was baiting him and he knew it. His eyes narrowed to a scowl. 'Old man?'

'Look in any mirror, Adam. The grey hairs are already there. Compared to me, you are positively over the hill and half-way down the other side.'

Jill spoke up for me. 'She's right about needing a guide, though. You don't have a lot of time.'

She suggested, quite logically, that the gang wouldn't hang around after today. They wouldn't want us to have time to get too organised. That gave us three hours until sunset, the time they'd probably make their escape to parts unknown.

'Thanks, Jill,' said Adam. He stared at her with one of those questioning looks of his that I could already recognise. 'You're an enigma, Constable Isherwood. I cannot believe you qualified as a police-woman, though obviously you did.'

'Thanks, Adam. But I'm not an enigma. I'm a Capricorn.'

★ ★ ★

We were using mobile phones for communication with Mick from now on. He was to be based at Huonville with Jill for the duration of the operation. Jill suggested the operational name 'Hunting Season'. It was as good as any.

Adam and I drove down in his rented four-wheel drive Ford Maverick. Most of the roads in the Glen Huon area were dirt. We didn't say much on the trip; I drove while Adam studied the detailed TASMAP plan of the area.

We crossed the Huon River and turned right onto Glen Huon Road, passing my grandparents and Lauren on the way. I was certain that the kidnappers didn't realise Lauren was there. It was simply a coincidence.

'Bruce at the general store would know if there were any strangers around his shop. It's off the beaten track so

161

chances are they're there, holed up.'

'Yeah. We'll go there but I'm not comfortable about taking you any closer. There is no way I need to worry about your safety too, Sandie.'

'Ah. I didn't know you cared,' I half-joked. He didn't think it was funny.

'Of course I care. You're gorgeous and you're brave. The way you saved that boy yesterday, and tackling Luigi at Barry's house — '

'That was Luigi? I owe him, big time. When I get my hands on him . . . '

Adam lost his cool at that moment, causing me to swerve then regain control.

'That's exactly what I mean, Sandie. You haven't got a clue about this situation and the danger. Damn. They'll have guns, same as me.' He patted the shoulder holster under his jacket. 'Just take me to this place in Lonnavale and after that leave it to the professionals.'

'OK, OK. I'll leave it to the professionals, Adam. Just make sure you don't get hurt.'

It was past eight when we arrived at Big Bruce's shop. He'd been there with his wife for twenty-odd years. I figured he'd be aware of comings and goings in the area.

The store was closed yet there were lights on out the back. Adam knocked on a dusty, cobweb shrouded window and a bloke with a bushy salt and pepper beard plus a pony-tail shoved the sash window up.

'We're closed. Push off.'

Adam showed his warrant card. 'Wait. I'm a Federal Police officer — '

'Mate. Yer could be Skippy, the bloody bush kangaroo. Don't matter none to me. For the last bloody time. Push off.'

I could see that Adam was out of his depth.

'Brucie. It's me. Sandie Ashton. Remember?' I flashed a smile at him.

'Sandie. Fair suck of the sauce bottle. Yer grown. Yer a sheila now and a blinking fit one too. No offence.'

'No offence taken, Brucie,' I replied. Bruce might have been the biggest chauvinist this side of the Black Stump, but he had a heart of gold and had been a good friend to Gran and Grandad over the decades. Like most things in Tassie, it took time for men to change to a more modern way of treating women.

'Mother. Look who it is! Little Sandie. Come on in and bring yer boyfriend with yer.'

'He's not my boyfriend, Brucie. I've got better taste than that. However, we do need your expertise.'

Bruce opened the fly-screen door gingerly. It was clinging to the door frame by one rusty hinge. From memory, it had been like that since 1984.

I did introductions before showing him the receipt that the crims had left in their car.

'I heard some strange sorts were moved in. Out on Woomera Road,' said Bruce's missus.

'Yeah. They came in here this morning. And I did notice a car parked

outside the old shearing shed when I was taking some pot plants to old Mrs Pickles. There was a bloke outside, locking up. Reckon that might be one of the yobbos ye're searching for.'

Bruce then gave Adam detailed directions. The shed was about four kilometres distant.

I promised to have a proper catch-up with Bruce and his wife before long. We thanked them for their help and rang Mick to arrange back-up.

Walking back to the 4X4, Adam commented, 'Nice couple. Fancy being kind enough to deliver pot plants to elderly residents.'

I giggled despite the situation facing us.

'When he said pot plants, he literally meant 'pot' plants, you dozy duck.'

'Marijuana?'

'It's a different way of life down here, Adam.'

'Yeah. I guess it is.'

I was about to get in the car to drive when Adam politely stopped me.

'Remember, Sandie. You stay here.'

Reluctantly I agreed. In spite of only meeting him properly for the first time yesterday, I had to admit I was attracted to Adam. I cared about him.

'You make sure you don't get hurt, Adam. Promise me.'

'I promise.' When I didn't seem convinced, he tried to reassure me. 'You can give me that Kiss of Truth if you wish. I won't object.' Adam puckered his lips and closed his eyes.

'Forget it. I'm trying to be serious here, Adam. Just . . . just don't take any chances, OK?'

I turned my back so he couldn't see the wetness in my eyes. He said he was turning off his phone to avoid it coming on while he was sneaking in to capture Luigi and Mad Dog. I waved goodbye and returned to Bruce's. It was fast becoming dark as the sun disappeared behind the mountains.

They welcomed me back and asked me what was happening. The excitement of a Federal Police operation was

a welcome distraction in the mundane life they led.

I had a thought about something Big Brucie had said about the shearing shed. I opened the folder with prints of Adam's photos, showing him one of Barry. He didn't recognise him.

'He wasn't one of the three blokes who came in here, Sandie.'

'Three?'

Adam expected to find and capture two of Magnus' gang. There was no possibility he'd be prepared for a third as well.

'Oh, hell. Adam's in major trouble. I need to warn him,' I exclaimed, desperately trying to call his mobile. No good. I recalled he said he was switching it off when he left me minutes earlier.

What could I do to save Adam? I was unarmed and not feeling good at all.

'Bruce. Can I borrow your truck?' I asked.

9

Bruce's truck was first cousin to a World War Two tank. She was solid and huge and loud. Everyone around this part of the Valley would be familiar with her, which was precisely what I was counting on.

Presumably the three criminals had been holed up in the shearing shed for a few days before attempting to kidnap Paula. Big Brucie's truck was one of those vehicles that would be regarded as part of the Glen Huon landscape.

On the plus side, I was certain they'd ignore her going past their hideout. At least I'd get an idea of what was going on with Adam and possibly help him. It was true that I hadn't worked out how but, as Gran used to say, 'Two steps at a time'.

There was a toggle switch on the dash labelled *Lights*. When I flipped it

on, the row of cab roof-mounted driving lamps illuminated the valley before me. Talk about overkill. Big, bad Bruce liked to be noticed at night obviously, as well as seeing everything for ten kilometres ahead of him. My drive-by wasn't going to go unnoticed.

I passed an incongruous Chinese-themed building with lantern lights peeking through its windows and turned my attention to the other side of the dirt road. There were lamps barely visible through the shutters of the ramshackle wooden structure. A dark sedan was parked outside. Either no one realised that the old shed had squatters or, more likely, no one around here cared. This part of the valley attracted people who often preferred life on the edge of civili-sation, without any rules and regulations. Someone once likened it to Tasmania's equivalent to *Deliverance* country.

I kept moving at a respectable pace. No point in arousing suspicion. Unfor-tunately there was no indication of Adam being inside and, if he were,

whether he was in control or otherwise.

Damn it! Looked like I'd have to double back and do a bit of snooping. Stopping a fair old way further down the track, I crept back along the tree line. There were voices from inside the shed. Adam's wasn't one of them.

The sounds were muffled and indistinct. Finding a loose board, I checked out the scene inside.

Adam was seated on a bale of hay. Three men stood around him, waving guns as they yelled at him. Although his hands weren't tied, there was no possibility of escape or overpowering them all.

Double damn!

Should I call in the back-up cars? Did Adam have enough time if I did? I thought not. It was up to me. And, quite frankly, I wasn't feeling great.

Running back to the truck, I contacted Mick to call in the troops while explaining my plan. When he said it was too dangerous for me, I explained exactly what I did in Sydney.

'Helping people. It's what I'm trained for.'

They were my final words to him as I fired up the truck and spun her around back to the shed. At the last moment as I went past, I yanked the wheel hard over. The shed was totally illuminated as I mentally apologised to Bruce for what was about to happen to his beloved 'girlfriend'.

It was about three metres from the road to the outer wall, through a barbed wire fence. The fence was crushed immediately. The old weatherboards splintered like matchwood under the powerful force of the truck and sheets of the rusted, galvanised-iron roof slid to the ground behind me. More importantly, the frightening sound of the destruction should have given the distraction Adam needed to react in his own way. He was only metres away from the new opening that was being created by the crash.

The truck screeched to a halt, as dirt, metal and wooden beams continued to crash all around us.

I breathed a sigh of relief. 'Well done, little truck. Now for stage two.'

The driver's door opened as I jumped out, making certain that the phalanx of flood-lights blinded every-one but me.

'What the . . . ?' Luigi emerged from the cloud of dirt on my right. He was rubbing his eyes from the dust and brightness. Also he was clearly angry.

'Sorry, mate. I swerved to avoid a kangaroo. Couldn't stop in time.'

Luigi was coming towards me at the same time as I wandered towards him. He had a gun held loosely in his hand, as he shielded his eyes.

As he moved into the shadows at the side of the truck, he stopped squinting.

'Wait. I seen you before.' He was becoming suspicious. There was still too much distance between us, though the dust was settling.

'Yeah — I work in Brucie's shop down the road,' was my response. *Just one more step, mate*, I calculated.

'Don't think . . . ' His eyes widened

as he remembered. 'You's that sheila from Chris' place.' His gun hand began to move.

I pivoted to deliver a powerful kick to his side with my right foot. It connected, jarring every bone in my body. Luigi grunted as the weapon flew from his grip towards the truck. I made an immediate grab for it as he struggled to regain his balance. Reaching it first I elbowed him in the face, before standing to level the gun at him.

'Stay down,' I told him, forcing him back to his knees. Moving back, I focused on the other end of the shed where Adam was grappling with someone. A shot ricocheted over my head from the truck's bright red bodywork so I took cover. Bruce was not going to be happy with what I'd done to his pride and joy — however, right this moment, that was the least of my problems.

Sirens were sounding outside as per my suggestion. Mad Dog, the bloke who'd shot at me, was dashing for the back door whereas the third guy was

wrestling with Adam.

I ran forward just as he punched Adam. He backed up, levelling the gun at Adam lying prostrate. Behind me, I heard Luigi run off and a door slam.

'Drop it,' I shouted at the thug. He didn't budge.

It was Darling Harbour all over again. The memories overwhelmed me for a second as I relaxed my grip. Instead of this brute, all I could see was a man standing there on the monorail bridge leading to Darling Harbour. He was pointing his gun at a teenage girl, having already wounded her boyfriend.

'Police. Drop your weapon,' I'd told him.

Slowly he'd turned his handgun towards me. I had to shoot, but I couldn't. I'd frozen and he shot me instead. The bullet that had passed through the fleshy part of my arm reminded me of that failure.

The stranger began to swing his weapon around to me, the motion accentuated by the huge shadows on

the shed wall behind him. That jarred me back to the present.

'Drop your weapon,' I shouted again, as I raised my own in a two-handed stance.

It was him or me. I fired.

He collapsed onto the hay-strewn floorboards, his weapon clattering to the side. I ran up to kick it to one side. He was screaming obscenities as he nursed his bleeding hand.

Outside I heard two motorbikes start up behind the shed.

Adam struggled to his feet and picked up his assailant's gun. 'Lucky shot.'

'Give me your handcuffs, Adam. And you,' I yelled at the criminal, 'roll over, hands behind your back.'

Adam stared at me as he passed the cuffs.

I passed him my weapon. 'Cover him.'

I knelt down to one side of the man and snapped the cuffs on him, avoiding the bloody but minor flesh wound. Two

armed officers entered from the front with their own weapons drawn.

'We're police,' I called out as we both raised our hands. 'One hostile in custody. The other two had motor-bikes.'

Adam turned to me. 'We're police? That's a surprise to me, Sandie Ashton.'

I shrugged.

'You can put your hands down, you two. We've been thoroughly briefed,' said the senior officer, turning to the other. 'Call it in, especially the motor-cycles. I want an ambulance and the Incident Team plus Forensics here right away. There's a doctor on standby.'

Thank goodness for that, I thought. *I can relax now*. I felt myself sweating yet cold inside. Then I felt a wave of weakness flow through my body as I collapsed onto the hay-strewn floor.

Hazily I felt Adam kneel by my side, lifting the sleeve of my blouse. He touched my forehead.

'She's burning up. Her arm's swollen and inflamed. I want another ambo

crew here ASAP.'

I opened my eyes to stare at his face only inches from mine, then closed them, hearing other cars arriving outside and footsteps all around. Had I been shot again? Didn't feel like it.

'Can't wait for the ambos. Get that doctor here. Right now,' I heard Adam shout just before I passed out.

10

'Good morning, Miss Ashton. You're in hospital. Good to see you're awake.'

I opened my eyes to a smiling nurse's face. I felt dreadful. When I tried to move my right arm, I felt the constriction of a blood pressure cuff along with bandages wrapped around a line into my arm.

Looking at the clear bag attached to the needle in my arm, I commented as clearly as I could.

'Hope that's neat gin. Could do with a drink.'

'Antibiotics. That infection did some serious damage.'

What infection? I wondered, deciding to lift my left arm. It resembled a mummy from one of those Hammer horror films. I guessed my gunshot wound wasn't healing as well as it should have.

'You had a sliver of glass in your arm

near the old bandage. On top of the bullet wound, the infected glass played havoc with your immune system. Didn't you realise?'

'Sort of. Other things on my mind.'

Yeah, like getting shot at by a psycho.

'Is this the same room as my sister . . . ?'

'Yes. Your sister was in here earlier this week. We've nicknamed it the Ashton suite and fitted a revolving door.' Her cheeky statement was reassuring. In my experience, nurses were only sarcastic with patients who were on the mend.

Mind you, I felt as crook as a dead chook; weak as a proverbial kitten. I made a mental note to learn some new metaphors . . . or was it similes?

'You said morning. Tuesday. What time?'

'Eleven o'clock. And it's Thursday. You were lucky. That boyfriend of yours was very concerned. Adam, I think that's his name.'

''S not my boyfriend,' I tried to say, as I closed my eyes. So sleepy.

'He sure acted like it. Good-looking bloke. You could do a lot worse, mark my words.'

* * *

By early afternoon, I was feeling more like a human. They'd taken the drip out and I'd been permitted to peel off those horrible sticky pads the heart monitor had been attached to. I also managed a trip to the en-suite bathroom for a long, hot shower, plus a change of clothes into garments with a lot more dignity. Call me old-fashioned but I preferred something that covered my rear end when I was wandering around.

At three thirty-five, Paula and Adam entered. Paula had flowers and Adam had a six-pack of Passiona and a mega-packet of Cherry Ripes.

'They suggested alcohol wasn't a good idea,' he said sheepishly. 'Paula told me you actually like this horrible passion-fruit concoction. I always thought you were weird and wonderful from the moment

180

we met on the plane.'

'Thanks, Mr Policeman, but don't think a few cans of soft drink are enough to make up for saving your miserable life. I expect a proper meal at a restaurant, at the very least. And not one called Macca's,' I replied.

He grinned. 'Like on a date?'

I glared at him. Paula broke in.

'You should have told me you weren't well, Sandie. Your arm was a real mess when they brought you in. The infection had spread everywhere. The doc said you're on the mend, thank goodness. You can come home this arvo. No more gunfights at the OK shearing shed for you for a while.'

I had to agree with her, grateful that she'd be there to care for me.

Adam put on his serious face.

'I have to say, Sandie, that you should have told us all you're a policewoman. It would have made life easier for everyone. That shot you made to disarm that bloke . . . it wasn't luck that you hit him in the hand, was it?'

'No. Despite my training, I didn't want to seriously injure him. We need any information he might have. As for not explaining I'm a Detective Constable — well, quite frankly, I didn't feel I was . . . not any more. That's why I came to Tassie. To decide if I'm still cut out to do police work.'

'It's to do with Darling Harbour, isn't it? I did some checking on you yesterday. I should have done it before — however I'd concentrated on Barry and his immediate family, not his stunning sister-in-law with her ratty hair.'

It was another questionable compliment. His own jet-black hair wasn't exactly haute coiffure.

'Whatever version you've heard about that day, it's not my version. It screwed me up, big time.'

Maybe this was what I needed to do; tell my story. For the first time since the clinical de-brief with the Investigation Unit, I felt up to getting it off my chest.

Adam and Paula each pulled up a

chair. Paula put her hand on mine.

I took a deep breath. This was going to be hard for me but it might be cathartic as well.

'We had a report of a guy menacing people on the walkway below the monorail track going from the city to the shopping complex at Darling Harbour. Along with some uniforms we headed down there. CCTV showed it was somebody my team had been investigating. Drug pushing.

'When we arrived, he was quite agitated and exhibiting threatening behaviour both to us and civilians. I managed to calm him down. Unfortunately when I called a uniformed officer to take him away, he failed to restrain him properly. Protocol was to cuff him, though that didn't happen. The bloke actually broke free, knocking the officer over after he took his weapon.'

'No wonder you weren't happy with uniformed officers — although it was just one guy who screwed up,' Paula reminded me.

'I was walking back to my fellow detectives. Then, all of a sudden, the situation which had been defused by me became a major incident. He started shooting at pedestrians on the walkway and the monorail trains passing overhead.

'I was about three metres away. He'd backed up to the edge of the bridge. Having warned him to drop the weapon, I faced him with my own gun drawn. Trouble was, I couldn't shoot. It was a second's hesitation yet it was long enough for him to attack me. I went down with a bullet in my shoulder. I could see his eyes as he aimed at me again. He was manic; maybe on drugs, I don't know for sure. My own gun had dropped when I fell so there was no possibility I'd survive a second shot. I was so scared . . . absolutely terrified. Reckoned it was the end for me.'

Adam's eyes were full of compassion. I sensed that he understood my emotions and my fear. He'd been in precisely the same predicament in the

shearing shed not three days earlier.

'One of my fellow detectives shot at him, he lost his balance and fell backwards into the water. He survived OK. No one was killed, fortunately, however the entire incident shook me up. Since that day, I've been second-guessing staying in the police, not because I was shot but because I failed to act when I should have. Sort of knocked the stuffing out of my self-confidence.'

It was hard to admit being a failure to myself as well as Adam and Paula.

Adam stood up and wandered over to the window. Some long overdue rain was falling over Hobart, streaming down the window that overlooked the city centre.

'You saved my life the other night, Sandie. What you did was reckless and stupid and very brave. From what I can see, you should continue in the police. You have skills far above other officers I've met. Deep down inside you're a copper, otherwise you wouldn't have

done what you did for me. I've already had a word to your superior back in Sydney. I need someone to help crack this case and I couldn't think of anyone better suited than you. We'll make a start this evening, if you wish. It's up to you, DC Ashton.'

Was I ready to go back to being a copper? I wondered. Truthfully, I realised I was. It was a relief that I'd faced down my fears and apprehensions.

'I've been doing a lot of thinking, lying here. And I've got a few ideas to track down Barry and that knife he stole. Tonight, you say? Six o'clock at police headquarters will suit me.'

For the first time in weeks, I felt like my old positive self. My body might need a bit longer to catch up, though. Jill had told me about the knife we would be searching for, and I now understood why the PM and a high-ranking Fed were involved.

Even so, I found it amazing that the knife actually existed. To my way of thinking, it was up there with the Easter

Bunny and the Tasmanian Triangle.

'Oh — I just remembered about the truck. Bruce is going to kill me.'

Adam laughed that Christmassy laugh of his.

'On the contrary. Bruce and that tank of his are local heroes. We'll call there tomorrow and you'll see for yourself.'

* * *

Paula returned to work at the same time as Adam made his excuses. He said he was sitting in on the interrogation of the bloke I'd shot, along with Jill and Mick. I suspected he'd seen through Jill's 'dumb bunny' act when she blurted out the name of the knife. In any case, he didn't make disparaging comments about her any longer.

When Paula kissed me on the head to say goodbye, he followed suit. It was a bit more awkward for him than for me, but I didn't object.

If he'd moved his lips a little lower to meet mine, I wouldn't have objected

187

either. Those eyes and that darkness of that shadowy hint of a beard on his olive skin were definitely growing on me. He smelled nice, too, like good-looking men are supposed to smell. No Eau de Dollar Shop here.

When Paula returned, I was changed and ready. Thank goodness my sister had brought me some trousers and a blouse as well as my other stuff. She was very subdued. Yours truly having been shot at twice in a few weeks obviously scared her . . . possibly more than it had me.

Instead, she talked about work. Things were looking up.

'That accountant bloke, Stephen, is definitely worth whatever we're paying him. He's uncovered quite a few more thousand of unpaid accounts. He's also found an intriguing conundrum; apparently there's an account not on the books where there's more than thirty thousand dollars hiding away. Either I'm going completely troppo or Holly's been salting monies from the business

away for herself.'

'Holly? I find that hard to contemplate, Paula. I only worked with her a few days yet I felt in my gut she was trustworthy. Are you certain?'

'The other errors and unpaid accounts could be put down to the antiquated system we've been using, and the fact that Holly has only been in the job for a short time. A lot of the accounts not chased up properly were from when I first opened up shop. It's not looking good as far as she's concerned.'

'Nevertheless, Paula, she's been pushing for this computer upgrade,' I reminded her.

'Not for a trained fraud investigator like Stephen to inspect things, though. He's got quite a pedigree, despite his unassuming nature.'

I had to agree with that. Some of the most evil people I'd met as a detective appeared like margarine wouldn't melt in their mouths. For too long I'd been involved with the seedier side of Sydney. I couldn't recall the last time I laughed

up there. Maybe Gran was right; a cat would be a welcome distraction at night when I went home.

★ ★ ★

Paula dropped me at Hobart Police Headquarters for our evening conference. I was taken straight to the room we'd been in before. A few officers recognised me from my involvement in the shearing shed drama and patted my back.

The first item on the agenda was an update on Barry and his pursuers. The prisoner's interrogation, after the medical treatment for his hand, was not very useful. Simply put, he didn't have a clue as to the identity of his boss, Magnus.

Furthermore he and his fellow crims were unaware of where Barry was. We'd already guessed as much. He'd been charged with attempted murder of a police officer.

Police on the mainland had tracked

down the individual who had told Magnus's gang about Barry's double fingerprint situation. Again, they couldn't identify Magnus's true name. The master thief was obviously paranoid about keeping incognito. No wonder he hadn't been caught.

'The only suggestion as to where Barry might be was that Southport receipt,' I explained. 'When I rang the pub, the girl who answered said she didn't recognise either Barry Denvers or Chris Davidson so that seems to be a dead end. And there's no sign of that car of his.'

Jill spoke up. 'Maybe we're not giving Barry enough credit. He's obviously clever enough to alter identities for himself. Possibly he's gone one step further.'

'Go on,' Adam said.

She paused. 'Do I have to pretend with you any longer? Mick and Sandie understand the truth about me and I reckon you worked it out too when I said the name of the knife.'

Adam gave her a reassuring nod. 'Go ahead, Constable. Must be difficult

hiding the real you with the dozy brunette act. I assume there's only a few other officers who realise you have a one hundred and fifty-plus IQ.'

'Some senior officers. As for the pretence, I actually enjoy being Bird-Brained Jill; she sees and hears much more than I ever could. Eventually the truth will come out, especially when I head up the promotion ladder.'

'What did we miss, Jill?' I prompted.

'Barry already has two identities. Why not have false plates on his car? We've been searching high and low for a particular number plate. We should be out there with a full description of the vehicle.'

Adam leaned back on his chair in realisation. The chair almost over-balanced, causing him to react quickly. Jill and I both sniggered.

'Makes sense,' he admitted graciously. 'Can you arrange that, Mick?'

Before departing, Mick asked a question that had been bothering me, too.

'Why hasn't Barry left Tasmania? I understand we have a watch order on

him for the main exit points although he could get out if he wanted. Shave off his beard. Dye his hair.'

'I've been thinking about that also.' Jill's face appeared to radiate concentration. 'Although Barry could leave Tassie, he'd be like a fish out of water on the mainland. This is his home and, as such, he can use that knowledge to evade us all . . . Magnus and the law.'

Maybe, I thought.

The high tech office phone on the desk rang. Adam answered it with a curt 'Hello. Superintendent Adam Powell . . . Wait. I'll put you on speaker.'

It was my boss, an Inspector in the New South Wales Police. Adam introduced us in turn, citing us as the Denvers Task Force. Mick excused himself.

It seemed he wished to address me primarily.

'Glad to hear you're recovering and are involved in tracking down Magnus and the artefact, Detective Constable. After Darling Harbour there were some concerns about your self-doubts. There

was never any question about your actions that day, regardless of what you thought. However I do have a confession to make. When I found out you were flying to Hobart, I bumped your flight.'

That was a surprise.

'I'm certain you had your reasons, sir.'

'Detective Constable, you have a gift for reading people. It amazes me how and I'm not the only one to notice. That's why we were concerned we might lose you after the shooting. I chose to delay your flight for a day because we had intel that Magnus would be on that flight. We . . . no, *I*, was hoping that your miraculous sixth sense might alert you to him on the plane as someone out of the ordinary. I gather that didn't work.'

'No, sir. The only person I noticed was Superintendent Powell. He was so uncomfortable in civie clothing, he stood out like . . . Sorry, sir. I thought he was a crim. To be fair, my head was

all over the place. You should have briefed me.'

'Possibly. I chose not to, in deference to your injury and state of mind. I thought you were more fragile than you obviously were. Now you realise the truth, I can only reiterate the importance of finding this Barry character, his stolen antiquity and catching Magnus. Can I ask, are you any closer? It is of extreme importance, as I'm sure you all understand.'

I yawned. Obviously I wasn't one hundred per cent yet. 'Yeah. But it'll have to wait till tomorrow.'

This woman had done enough for one day, I decided. What difference could a few hours make?

If only I'd known then how wrong I would be.

11

Until we had more information, there was little we could do in the search for Barry. We chose to check if there were any further clues in the shearing shed, ones that might be more evident in daylight.

Adam and I set off at eight a.m. heading towards the Huon Valley. As I drove, I took some pleasure in a running commentary for Adam. He'd confessed earlier that this trip was his first to the Apple Isle. He'd studied Australian history and geography in school and had a rudimentary knowledge of Australia's second oldest capital city, Hobart, and our state. I explained how it was originally called Van Diemen's Land after some long-dead Dutch bloke.

He was impressed by the landscape.

'Every corner seems to bring a new

postcard vista. It's impressive. Out in the Glen Huon Valley, it reminded me of a vision I've had since my childhood; the Garden of Eden. I'm sure you can understand that.'

I found myself agreeing. 'What's more, there are snakes and apples, like from the Tree of Life.'

'And me with a name like Adam . . . shame your name isn't Eve instead of Sandie. Just think of us wandering around the forests, naked.'

I had to swerve to keep the car from heading towards a ditch.

'Don't even think about me in that way, please. I might be horrible and ugly without clothes on . . . and so might you.'

It was a vain protest, I suspected. Moreover there was no possibility that I'd ever tell him my second Christian name was Evelyn. A real life Adam and Eve in the Tassie bush?

'Are you blushing, Sandie?'

'No, just a bit hot. I need one of those soft drink cans, please.' I pulled into a parking area on the side of the

road. Although I was aware of his constant glances while I drank, I fixed my eyes straight ahead.

The Huon Highway was lined with apple orchards and, unlike the Midlands, was quite green. Huonville hadn't changed that much since I grew up around there. The cinema had closed, which was a shame. I had my first kiss there.

We crossed the bridge but turned right towards Belvoir House and Big Brucie's store. I wanted to see them both. I was glad Adam had hired a comfortable car this time; we'd probably do a hundred-plus k today. It was a good thing the days were long this time of the year. Night driving often involved nocturnal animals like devils, bandicoots or possums running across the roads.

I believed there was nothing super-urgent about searching for Barry. Finding him was still a long shot. Besides, all of Tassie's police force were assisting. I wanted to visit my gran and grandad to reassure them. No doubt the events out west would be the talk of the valley. I

wished to see Lauren too.

Grandad made us welcome straight away. Despite protestations that we'd eaten, some pumpkin scones and lamingtons were quickly produced, along with coffee and tea.

Gran came in from the garden, cleaned herself up and joined us. In retrospect I should have realised what would happen next. Gran must have been absent when the Good Lord was handing out subtlety genes.

'Hello, you two. Sandie, can't you sort out that hair of yours? Appearances are important, my girl.' Gran turned her gaze to Adam, giving him a thorough once-over. She touched his cheeks before running her hands over his muscular chest. Adam didn't move.

'Who is this handsome young man? Don't tell me you have a new boyfriend already? You only had your last one arrested on Monday.'

Adam grinned.

'Gran. This is Adam Powell. He's not my new boyfriend. And Gareth wasn't

199

my boyfriend either. Just some thieving, brainless magpie I went out with one time.'

I gave her my most evil glare, willing her to be quiet. It didn't work.

'Adam? Adam? Don't recall the name but I do recognise you from Sandie's description. You're that bloke from the plane that she said she liked the look of but she reckoned you were dodgy underneath. Is that you?'

'Gran! I never said he was dodgy,' I protested vehemently.

'It's OK, Sandie. I suppose I am a bit dodgy and your charming granddaughter did meet me on the plane. And in a break-in at Barry's home . . . and, oh yes, when she saved my life at some disgusting, smelly shearing shed the other night.'

'Oh, that was you? Heard all about it. Wrecked old man Mullen's shed, though. Course he's been dead for twenty years, so don't reckon he'll complain much. Adam, you say. Like in the Garden of Eden. Sandie's second name is Eve. Well,

Evelyn actually. I suppose she told you that.'

'No,' Adam replied with a wry laugh. 'How interesting. Perhaps Eve and I could go for a walk in the forest sometime? Eat an apple or two?'

I was fuming. Gran had totally destroyed my credibility. Was it a family conspiracy? First Paula, now Gran. I threw my arms up in the air, screamed in frustration, then stormed out in a huff.

I did overhear their parting remarks.

'She's always been highly strung,' Gran explained. 'I hope you realise what you're letting yourself in for.'

'Yes, Mrs Avalon. You have a gorgeous granddaughter. Apart from her hair, of course.'

*　*　*

When we left Belvoir House around ten, Adam was very complimentary about my family. I didn't feel the same, especially about Gran. How could she drop me in it like that?

201

For the most part, we drove in silence. Adam wanted to examine the place where he almost died for clues. I didn't understand how he could do that until we entered the derelict remains. Surprisingly, it was reasonably intact, despite my destructive efforts with the truck. Forensics had been there, finding very little that could help us.

He made his way carefully across the debris to the hay bale where he'd sat with that firearm pointed at him. I followed discreetly.

'Just thinking how close I came to . . . you know. Gets you thinking. Funny thing, they say your life flashes before your eyes but mine didn't. Maybe because I don't have a life outside of work.'

I took a seat at his side.

'Join the club. Gran suggested I get a cat. At least there'd be something to come home to apart from a microwave meal or a takeaway.'

We looked at one another. There was a loneliness in his eyes that I could relate to.

The moment was interrupted by the sound of some animal scurrying across the floor.

'Anything to worry about?' Adam asked.

'No. Tassie's very safe. Just the snakes. Oh, and the jack-jumpers. They're bitey ants. That noise was probably a Tasmanian tiger.'

'Tasmanian tiger? I thought they were extinct?'

I dusted myself off, giving him a wink. 'Don't believe everything you hear, Superintendent. Tassie still has lots of secrets.'

Adam paused, taking my hands in his. 'You do understand that I find you extremely attractive, Sandie. You're smart and brave and feisty.'

He leaned across to kiss me. It was perfectly natural. We'd almost been killed in this place but we'd survived, working together. Perhaps there should be good memories of this shed to negate the bad ones.

I savoured the light touch as our lips brushed then parted, once, twice . . .

then he pressed his mouth to mine and I felt his arms enfold me with the kind of caring strength I'd longed for all my life.

When we drew back, he let his fingers play with strands of my hair, drawing it across my cheek.

'I love you, Miss Ashton,' he whispered, softly.

I took a deep breath, my mind awash with emotions and logic battling to take control of my own voice. Then I heard a third voice. My heart.

'I love you too, Mr Powell. Very, very much.'

* * *

We arrived at Big Brucie's Emporium around ten-forty. It was a strange place that sold all sorts to the locals in this isolated part of the Valley. The Huon River was quite narrow here. Further down towards the sea, it was well over four k wide. Outside the iconic store was a picnic area by a rivulet that gurgled its

way to the Huon. A basic kiddies' playground boasted two tyre swings, a climbing frame and a slippery dip, nestled alongside a rusting yellow Vauxhall Victor.

Bruce did take-aways for those who didn't mind the odd touch of botulism. Cleanliness wasn't one of his strong points although, to be truthful, there had never been any complains to the Health Department of Huon Council; at least none I was aware of. The cemetery over the other side of the stream might have explained that. What did they say? Dead men tell no tales.

'G'day, Sandie. Mr Fed.' Bruce came out from the shade of the shop, not bothered by the blazing sun. Adam and I both wore broad-rimmed Akubra hats and sunnies that offered some protection.

Scowling at Adam and me, he beckoned us over to his poor old truck. I gritted my teeth. Bruce had a temper on him like a swarm of wasps.

'You certainly stuffed her up good

and proper, didn't you, Sandie? Blinking bullet holes, too. Hope he was worth it.' He nodded towards Adam. I felt my cheeks flush red.

Adam was about to take responsibility and offer to pay for repairs when Bruce broke into a smile the size of a Tassie devil's mouth.

'Just pulling-yer legs, youngsters. Me and me truck. We're famous now. Even had a reporter ring me from Leeds in Scotland ... or was it Wales? Never mind.'

He went on to explain that the number of visitors to his shop had rocketed, cleaning him out of ice creams and snacks. People were eager to see the famous vehicle with all her damage so Bruce was adamant that he didn't want her repaired. He'd already had photos taken with 'the beast', him and the shed, and was considering selling them as postcards.

'There's a picture plus an interview in this week's local paper. Full colour, too. Reckon we might even get ourselves on the tourist route. All them

coachloads of Mainlanders with money? Can't be bad. Tell yer what. I'll give yer a paper with the pics in it. Won't even charge yers for it. Now . . . when I signs it, do yer want it *To Sandie and Adam, with love*?'

★ ★ ★

We couldn't escape fast enough after that. To be fair, I was pleased for him. If our adventure helped Bruce, that was a great thing.

It did break the silence between Adam and me. We discussed lots of things as we drove back to Hobart. Unfortunately a part of my logical thinking began nagging at me, warning me that I shouldn't get too involved.

Adam worked for the Feds. He was based in Canberra. I worked for the New South Wales police, based in Sydney. There was almost three hundred kilometres between the two capitals.

A long-distance love affair? It didn't bode well.

As we approached our state capital, I decided to have a quick squizz at what they'd written about the shearing shed siege. Two paragraphs into the narrative made me gasp in shock. How could they be so stupid?

'Adam. Pull over. Quick. Read this.' I handed him the paper open on the front page article and photo. He swore then apologised. We had a big problem.

'Already on it,' he said, lifting out the mobile we used for comms. The crim we'd locked up had admitted that his mates were monitoring police band communications. Adam stepped outside under the shade of a huge ghost gum, while I reread the terrifying section of the Brucie's narrative.

'Policewoman Sandie Ashton drove my truck through the shed wall. Sandie grew up in Tasmania and her grand-parents, the well-known Charlie and Freda Avalon, still live locally at Belvoir House.'

Talk about a major breach of security.

Adam and I could see that Lauren was the weak point in this continuing drama. With Barry well and truly off the radar, there was a slim possibility of either Magnus or us finding him.

Taking Paula from her car was a mistake; Barry wouldn't come out of hiding with the artefact for his ex-wife. On the other hand, if they could kidnap his daughter, then Barry would do anything to save her.

Paula, Adam and I had discussed this and concluded that Lauren would be safest for the foreseeable future at Gran's and Grandad's. They had a different surname to Ashton, with only a few people in Hobart realising that Paula had relatives in the Huon. It was the perfect place to keep Lauren incognito.

Until now.

Adam jumped back into the driver's seat.

'Change of plan, Sandie. We're

heading back to Huonville. Police have been dispatched to your grandparents' home. Now, if you don't mind, I might break a few speeding laws.'

I set about ringing Grandpa on my own mobile to warn him. No answer. As we sped back down into the valley, I kept trying, becoming more and more concerned. Finally, a female voice answered. It wasn't Gran.

'This is the police. Who are you and what do you want?'

'It's DC Ashton here. Is everything OK?'

There was lots of speaking in the background. Grandad came on the line. 'Sandie? The police are here now but it was too late. I'm sorry.'

'Too late?'

'Two men came with guns. They've taken them, Sandie. They've taken your Gran and Lauren.'

12

'Did you hear me, Sandie? Those men from the shearing shed . . . they've kidnapped both of them.'

'I heard you, Grandad. We're on our way back to you.'

'What . . . How can I tell Paula? I can't. She trusted us. I tried to stop them . . . fight them off.'

'Grandad. It's not your fault. I'll tell Paula. Pass me back to the police-woman, please. And don't worry. We'll get them back, safe and sound.'

I spoke to the young officer who was at Belvoir House along with a number of other police and ambos. Although Grandad had taken a nasty blow to his head apparently, he seemed OK.

Roadblocks had been set up. They hadn't worked when Paula was almost captured, so I doubted they'd work now.

The two gangsters had left a note with

their demands and a mobile number. It was untraceable. The normal methods of tracking weren't any use. Explaining that the villains had military training seemed to solve that puzzle.

Before I rang Paula, I made Mick and Jill aware of the situation, asking them to collect Paula. She would be in no state to drive out to our family homestead alone.

Finding Barry was now a priority in addition to rescuing my family. I imagined Magnus's gang would want a state-wide appeal for Barry to surrender himself to them along with the knife. And they'd give him a deadline . . . otherwise nasty things would happen to his little girl.

I took a phone call from Jill. The main Tassie newspaper had been contacted by Magnus, exactly as I'd expected; maximum publicity to draw Barry out from hiding. Telly stations too. It did depend on how undercover he was, though. Newspaper and television appeals for him wouldn't help if he was holed up in a tent or cave in the middle of nowhere.

Telling Paula was the hardest thing I'd ever had to do. It was much worse as I had to do it by phone. I didn't have the luxury of driving to Hobart in order to break the news in person. By the time we were finished, I heard Holly calling out that there were reporters on the other phones. Happily Jill and Mick had arrived by then.

★ ★ ★

Adam really put his foot down. Fortunately traffic was light and much of the highway was straight. He had a grim, determined expression, reminding me of his appearance on the plane.

'On the flight the other day, you were searching for Magnus, weren't you? The same tip-off that my boss had.'

'For all the good it did me. How can you recognise a master criminal when there's no info about him, apart from a pseudonym? No idea of age, where he was born, photos, fingerprints; it's like catching a shadow, Sandie. The number

of years the Federal Police have been after him. We can't let him steal that knife. We simply can't.'

Passing Mountain River, a police patrol car pulled out from a side road, siren and lights on.

'Oh, great,' said Adam, slowing down. The cruiser pulled alongside indicating that we should follow them. Adam waved back.

'They're not pulling us over,' he explained. 'They're running interference for us instead.'

He accelerated to keep pace. Even so, the time to get to Belvoir House was still ages.

I dashed inside to check on Grandad while Adam questioned the attending officers and detectives. Kidnapping was one thing — though stealing a child was far, far worse in the eyes of the Tasmanian authorities.

Grandad was shaken. The cut to his forehead had been dressed. He was sipping hot tea that someone had prepared for him. Although I was certain that

he'd given his account of what had transpired, he was keen to tell me too.

'When I heard a car pull up outside . . . '

I stopped him as Paula came running in through the front door and down the gallery to the family room where we were seated. She and the two police from Hobart all needed to hear too.

The following minutes were a jumble of hugs and questions about Grandad's state of health as well as tears of anguish. When we were ready for the story, Paula had calmed down enough to take it all in. In the absence of any other clue, I believed she held the location of Barry somewhere in her subconscious. She knew him better than anyone. Paula needed to be strong and focused if we were to bring our family back together.

'Like I was telling Adam and Sandie, I thought it was them two coming back when I heard the car pull up out front. Lauren was down here, reading that magic Larry Potter book of hers. However once

215

I opened the door, I realised things wasn't right. Two blokes, it was. Mean-looking too. They pushed their way in, even with me trying to stop them. I'm not as strong as I used to be. They asked where Lauren was. Even had a photo of her with that Barry bloke and her mum. I threatened to call the police. They pushed me over then ripped the phone right off the wall. That's when I felt my old heart acting up.' He took a moment to catch his breath.

'Lauren must have heard the commotion. She came running down the gallery and laid into those two men with her feet and fists for all the good it did. They laughed at her trying to help me. Then the big one — Mad Dog, the Italian one called him — he raised his fist to whack poor little Lauren across the head.'

I heard Paula's painful gasp.

'But he didn't,' I prompted Grandad with a sideways glance to my distressed sister.

'No. The other fella told him not to

touch her, otherwise Magnus would hear about it.' Paula relaxed a little. 'Anyways that Mad Dog bloke backed off. He started telling her to stop whacking him otherwise he'd hurt me. That made her stop. She crouched down to help me sit up against the wall. I could see why he was called that nickname; he was salivating all the time like he had that rabies thingy. That's when your gran came in the back door. She didn't suspect anything. Hearing's not so good these days.

'Anyways she started waving some secateurs around until one of them threatened me and Lauren. She dropped them straightaways then. Guess she understood none of us could stop these men from doing whatever they wanted.'

'What happened next, Mr Avalon?' Jill's voice was soothing as she held Grandad's trembling hand. That seemed to calm him a little. Mick filled Grandad's empty cup with more tea, adding three teaspoons of sugar. Jill passed him the cup.

Grandad stared into her eyes, drawing strength from her. I began to see yet another aspect to her complex personality.

'They bound our hands behind our backs with the tie-back thingy from those velvet curtains over there, put the note down and told me Barry better deliver the goods or he'd never see little Lauren again. That's when your gran yelled out something none of us expected. She suggested taking her as well and that she wouldn't be no trouble.'

I believed we all understood at that moment, how brave and strong my gran was. Not only could she be there to help a terrified child with the trauma, she could be some sort of restraining buffer between the thugs and Lauren.

'The Italian one was the brains, it appeared. Said yeah, to take your gran as well. In his words, 'Someone to control the brat.' To be fair, Lauren had been sobbing away for ages. Before the four of them left they allowed your gran to give me a kiss goodbye. That's when

she whispered about her phone being in her apron.'

I sat up. 'You can trace her phone. Why didn't someone tell us this before?'

Mick explained. 'Because her clever plan didn't work, Sandie. Once our officers arrived and freed your grandad, he informed them about the phone. Luigi and Mad Dog must have searched your gran, found the phone and sent us off on a wild goose chase. We traced the signal to Cygnet in the back of some farmer's ute.'

Damn. My hopes disappeared. Of course the men weren't stupid.

Adam was keen to have some idea of their plans.

'Mr Avalon. Sorry to interrupt but time is of the essence. I've read the note they left. Was there anything they said to each other which may suggest where they were taking them?'

My grandfather paused, apparently revisiting the entire traumatic experience in his mind. Last time, when they snatched Paula, they wanted us to find

their hideout because they intended to kill Adam. This time they had a different agenda, one dictated by Magnus to force Barry to come forward. Magnus could then steal the ancient object that Barry had hidden for years. I doubted the kidnappers would let anything slip about their own place of shelter this time.

Grandad shook his head in frustration. I could sense his mounting anger.

I gently nudged him, conscious that we could push his fragile body too much. 'Anything about their clothes? The way they behaved? Did they have some distinctive smell like eucalyptus or pine or . . . '

His eyes opened wide. 'Smoke. The big one. He stank. Body odour — but smoke too.'

Adam sat forward on the crowded settee.

'There were smudges on the note of demands they left on the kitchen bench.' He stood to speak to some forensics woman. They'd bagged the original and

copied it for our team as well as other officers.

Returning to us, he confirmed that the smudges appeared to be from charcoal.

'Assuming that the black carbon and distinctive smell wasn't from a barbie or some fireplace, perhaps they've been in a bushfire zone. I'm not a local. Are there any bushfires at present?' His gaze was directed at Mick and Jill, the most likely ones to be aware of all emergency situations.

'None at present, Adam,' Mick said. 'There was a big one on South Bruny Island last week. Mainly scrub land and forests.'

Paula's expression perked up a little. 'I recall that Bazza had some books about Bruny at his home. Come to think of it, they aren't there now. Maybe Barry took them?'

'Or Luigi,' I suggested. 'Trying to track him down? Either way that gives us some idea.'

'Bruny Island. I don't recognise the

name,' said Adam. I left to grab a map from the study wall, brought it back and pointed.

'It's possible Magnus and his henchmen tracked him down to there. When they couldn't find him over there, Magnus had one last option. Kidnap Lauren.'

Grandad and Paula were both very agitated. I decided it was best if Adam, Mick, Jill and I discuss the logistics away from them. We made our excuses to move outside into the shade of the magnolia, to a table and chairs. Fortunately the ever-present flies weren't too bad.

Adam asked us about the copies of Magnus's demands that we each had been given. They were neatly printed and grammatically correct so it was fair to assume Magnus had written the original even though the only fingerprints on it were those of Luigi. It appeared Magnus was continuing to be his secretive self, leaving it possible to walk away if any of his underlings were captured.

I read my copy once again, urgently

seeking any hint about where Gran and Lauren might be.

Dear Coppers,
   You have until midnight tonight to bring me Chris Davidson and the knife or we hurt his precious daughter. I suggest you put it on the news. No Chris equals no pretty little girl any longer.

Not surprisingly, it was unsigned.
They were using the name Chris for the man I knew as Barry.
Adam was senior officer and co-ordinator. He began by addressing Jill and Mick.
'Your bosses agree with me that we should use the media to put out an appeal. I'd prefer not to use Paula as yet. From what she says, Barry dotes on Lauren so simply the threat of harm to her should draw him out of hiding.'
'Would he risk his own life for his daughter?' Mick asked me.
'Ordinarily I would say so, yet he's not the man I thought he was. Therefore, who knows. From what I've seen

223

and heard, he loves her a lot. Adam, do you think they'd actually harm Lauren or is it just an empty threat? You're more aware of those two crims than anyone here. After all, you were the guy that caught them, weren't you?'

The Federal officer considered that for a moment. 'They're unpredictable and they've done bad things, including murder. Despite his size and name, Mad Dog is more into bluster than physical violence. Considering his build, most people wouldn't want to fight him in any case. He's easily talked into doing the wrong thing whether it was stealing precious statues from the Middle East or doing what he's doing now. I'm convinced that neither he nor Luigi have any idea who they work for. They didn't appear to when they were arrested years ago trying to smuggle goods into Australia. I doubt that's changed. Magnus is far too secretive. I . . .'

He scrunched up his copy of the demand, grimacing in anger, before silently standing to wander over to the

trunk of the tree. His hands were clenching and relaxing over and over.

Sensing his intense frustration, I went to him.

'Adam. Walk with me.' I took one of his hands. He was trembling. I assumed that Mick and Jill realised that there was a problem and I was doing my best to solve it. They had other avenues they could pursue in the current massive state-wide search.

I slowly led Adam towards the tranquil area surrounding the dam. He'd been pushing himself too much. Moreover I suspected some delayed reaction from the incident at the shed. No one could blame him for that, yet perhaps he had stronger expectations about his own inner strength. He needed a friend now. I doubted he'd ever had one before.

He was quiet, though the tension and anger were still there.

As we sat on the bench overlooking the rippling waters on the dam, I gently broached my concerns. He stared at

something on the water.

'I'd ask if you were OK, except you'd probably yell, 'Of course I am, you stupid woman. Leave me alone.''

He let go of my hand. 'I'd never call you 'stupid'. You are one of the strongest, most remarkable people I've met. If we weren't so embroiled in this huge mess . . . ' He didn't finish but the expression on his face told me what he would have said.

'Unlike you, I don't have a loving family, Sandie . . . at least, those that I've met. You might live in Sydney, yet Tasmania is obviously your home. This situation with Lauren . . . well, it's bringing back some painful memories to me. I had a younger sister who was killed in a car accident when she was seven.'

'That's so sad. Could I ask her name?'

Adam seemed reluctant to answer. Was I intruding too much?

'Laurel,' he said at last. 'I was three years older than her, always looking out for her as a big brother does. When she

died, I guess a part of me died too . . . the emotional part. I joined the Army, then the Feds. Relationships have always been a problem with me. With work colleagues . . . with girls and women also.'

His confessions were interrupted by a flight of sulphur-crested cockatoos passing raucously overhead.

'Same with me. If you remember, I mentioned that Gran suggested that I buy a cat to share my life with. Perhaps we could share one together.' I didn't mean to say it like that but I did.

The next step felt so natural. I leaned across to kiss him tentatively. He responded, becoming more passionate as he embraced me.

When we eventually parted, he appeared confused.

'That shouldn't have happened, Sandie. Especially not here . . . not now.'

I touched his cheek. 'That's not true. We both need to be focused on finding Barry, Lauren and my gran. We can't afford to waste energy on not trusting

one another or denying the affection we feel for one another. I'm tired of being alone. So are you, Adam. Now we can solve this together. Come on, let's go back to see what's happening. Besides, this is a black spot for phone reception.'

We set off hand in hand. Adam checked his phone when I passed it back.

'You knew that was a dead zone for communication?'

'Of course. You needed some time to yourself. You were no use to anyone like you were. Think of it as ten minutes R and R.'

At that moment, Adam's mobile rang.

'It's Hobart.' He put it on loud speaker.

'A traffic warden reported that car you're searching for, Superintendent. It's in the Kettering ferry car park.' A detailed description was given with the warden told to keep a tactful eye on it and report any developments.

Adam turned to me after disconnecting.

'Does that make sense?'

I considered all the facts and speculation. 'Yes, it does. The smoky smell on the two who kidnapped my family indicated being near a bushfire on Bruny Island, and Kettering is where the Bruny Island ferry sails from. Barry might be around there. We should check it out. It's about fifty minutes drive from here.'

Catching Barry was the first step, but I realised we might resolve this case once and for all.

Jill and Mick were running towards us, weaving between the masses of fruit trees and wattles.

'Kettering,' I yelled. 'Barry's at Kettering.'

'That's not why we're here,' Mick called back. 'Your grandad. They think it's a heart attack.'

13

Adam and I sprinted towards Belvoir House, closely followed by Mick and Jill. The ambos were still there from earlier. That was good.

As we arrived at the front door, I could see them wheeling my grandfather out to the ambulance. Paula was standing by, her clenched fist held to her mouth. I ran up to her.

'What happened, Paula?'

'After you left he was fine at first. The paramedics came to check he was OK before they left. Said his blood pressure was too low. That's when he began to complain about chest pains. He appeared disoriented and his skin was clammy. They gave him an ECG and some of that nitroglycerine spray under his tongue. That helped. He's off to hospital to see what the problem is. On top of everything that's gone on, I

230

couldn't bear to lose him.'

'We'll follow them to the hospital,' I suggested, not thinking that Paula's car was still at Hobart. Mick had driven her here.

'No, Sandie, I need you to do the job you're trained to do. Find Lauren. Find Gran. I'll go in the ambulance.' I hesitated. 'Please, Sandie. Go.'

'Just make sure you keep me posted, Paula.'

'I will, kid. He's in good hands.'

I kissed Grandad, hugged Paula and went to see the others. Adam had informed them of what we had discovered about Barry's whereabouts.

Mick made a decision. 'We'll take two patrol cars. They're faster. You go with Jill, Sandie. Adam can come with me. Let's get going.'

I decided that it was a sensible move splitting our teams up. Obviously Adam and I weren't permitted to drive Tasmanian marked police vehicles — and we could use this opportunity to share information gathered by each pair.

The first priority was to find Barry, inform him of the threats to both Lauren and Gran then formulate a plan to resolve this nightmare. If I could manage it in any possible way, Magnus would answer for what he'd done to all of us.

Although it may have been a little faster on the main highway heading towards Hobart, Mick opted for the quieter route bypassing the port of Cygnet, over the hills then up the coast road to the ferry terminal and marina at Kettering.

Despite her youth, Jill was a capable driver of the powerful Ford Futura. She kept up with Mick as we roared past the apple orchards outside Cygnet. Seeing signs for the local college, I was reminded about Jill's confession. She'd suggested that I'd helped her choose to be a copper all those years before at school.

I reminded her about it.

She effortlessly negotiated some sharp bends as we passed through the township, accelerating again while she explained. 'I never fitted in at school. Guess I was too eager to show off in class. Even at

seven, the other kids stayed well away from me at playtime. A few of their older sisters decided to pick on me just for fun. The boss girl was called Big Patty. Do you remember me yet, Sandie?'

'Not you. I remember Patty, though. Her gang ran that playground. Extorting money from other kids, stealing watches and trainers. Patty's Peacocks . . . strutting around the schoolyard, bullying everyone they could.'

They weren't pleasant memories.

'I wore glasses back then. My hair was quite blonde, like yours is now. I was short, and timid with older kids. Looked like a geek long before they invented the word.'

I'd blocked a lot of memories from that time.

'There was a pathetic girl in Miss Tangy's class. She exuded that victim aura; you know. 'Here I am, everyone. Please pick on me. I won't fight back.' Wasn't you, though. Her name was Henrietta. Poor little Henrietta.'

Jill glanced across at me as we climbed

the hill, leaving the Huon Valley behind. Mrs Thirlstone's washing was still hanging on a line across her front veranda, just as it had fifteen years ago.

'Jill's my second name. Haven't used Henrietta since 1998.'

'Oh, hell. It was you. I should have done something earlier. I didn't realise . . . I'm so sorry.'

Jill laughed. 'You never did horrible things to me, you silly sausage. It was the others, Patty and those twins. In fact it was you who told them to leave me alone, despite there being three of them and one of you. You stood up for me and they beat the tar out of you for doing it. You ended up in hospital. Concussion, they said. And you never came back to our school. Eventually I heard your family moved to Sydney.'

'Dad told me I was uncontrollable. He never listened to me when I tried to explain what had gone on. He was ashamed of me.'

'I don't have any idea about that, Sandie. I do owe you, though. You stood

up to Patty in front of me and a lot of the school. That inspired me until, years later, I chose to join the police to help people like you did. Patty and the other girls were expelled for what they did to you. I wrote to thank you before you moved to Sydney. Did you get it?'

'There was a note. Dad screwed it up saying it was a mistake. No one would thank me because I was so evil. No one liked me, he kept saying. I can't believe that he and Mum would lie to me . . . just because I was growing up and showing independence.'

He had wanted to control me by destroying my self-confidence. What father would do that to their child? I was certain that Paula and my grand-parents were given a warped version of the truth; evil Sandie was there in my father's lies.

I began to sob at the recollection of all of those lectures from Dad that were so very, very wrong. He'd stifled my independence for his own selfish reasons.

Jill became concerned. I told her I'd be OK and thanked her for reminding me that I wasn't the horrible girl that I'd believed.

By the time our small convoy reached the main north-south highway running alongside the Derwent River, I was in control again. I dared not look at the state of my face in the rear vision mirror. Instead I blew my nose noisily.

Mike switched off the sirens as we approached the Kettering turn-off. I was feeling more like my old self. I needed to focus on the present to rescue my family.

* ★ ★

When I'd left Tassie, Kettering was only a small marina. It had changed a lot. There were piers with boats tied up everywhere, plus loads anchored in the small bay. Great.

Once we arrived in the large parking lot, Jill had a quick word with Adam. I gave my own quick version of what had

happened in the car and my father's actions back then. No wonder my return to Tassie had caused me to have so many mixed-up feelings. Finally I wiped my eyes again.

'Is my hair all right?' I asked Adam.

'Messy and sticking out everywhere. No change at all. Just the way I like it.' He kissed my forehead affectionately.

Jill's stern voice interrupted us. 'Oi. You two. You're not in one of those old fashioned drive-in movie places. Besides I thought you oldies were well past all that sort of behaviour.'

'Oldies,' I scoffed. 'I'm only twenty-six.'

'Yeah. Like I said. Old.' She gave me a wink.

* * *

Paula rang through to tell me that Grandad was fine. It seemed his heart problem was one that could be controlled with medication. That was such a relief. I passed the good news on,

taking a deep breath to focus myself on the task at hand.

Taking some binoculars from the trunk, Mick scanned the parking lot.

'Yes. There's Barry's car, exactly where we told it would be. Trouble is, there's no sign of the guy himself. Maybe he took the ferry over to the island and is lying low. Or perhaps he's in some B&B here. Where do we start?'

Adam made a decision. 'Some low-profile chat to the ferry staff? Do you guys have any civvies with you? Uniforms might scare Barry off.'

The two uniformed officers grabbed some bags from one of the boots and were about to go change when I stopped them.

'There's another possibility. Somewhere a lot more obvious for him to be staying.'

Jill was first to pipe up. 'The yachts! That might be where he was down at Southport, too.'

Adam agreed. 'Worth checking out. Let's pray that Barry's on board his

boat. There aren't many shops around, and it seems all of his other bolt holes have been compromised. Hobart Central hasn't been contacted by him so, unless he doesn't care for his daughter, I doubt he's heard our appeal for coming forward to save her. We have to find him somewhere here. Any ideas?'

I'd been thinking things through.

'Jill and Mick. Could you go check the ferry staff as well as the ones in the gift shop and restaurant? Oh, and is there someone like a harbour master monitoring the boats in the marina? Just show them Barry's photo. Adam and I will start examining these boats.' I judged the vast number moored there. 'We might be some time.'

As our companions headed off to the modern terminal at the side of the car boarding ramp for the car ferry, we made a start. It was daunting.

'You're a bloke. Any idea what we're looking for? Big boat? Sails? Colour? Name even?'

Adam shrugged. 'Haven't a clue. A

boat's a boat. Maybe Mick can get an idea from Barry's photo — though I reckon, with all this unwanted attention, he'll change his looks as often as I change my underwear.'

'I sincerely hope that you are more regular than that, Mr Powell.'

The glare from the sparkling water would have been quite hard to look at without the polarising lenses in my sunnies. It was hot, and there was little sea breeze to cool us down.

It wasn't the weekend as yet, so the numbers of part-time sailors weren't high. That was one good thing. However there were loads of tourists wandering around awaiting the ferry. They'd tired of the gift shop, I guessed, and were soaking up the ambience of this peaceful location.

We began to make our way along the wooden walkways that had boats moored on either side. I was grateful that my powers of processing information about my surroundings were working again. That situation on the plane when I'd

completely misread Adam was a blip. True, I'd identified him as someone pretending to be different — but to regard him as a someone to be afraid of? How could I have been so wrong?

My mind was subconsciously absorbing sights, sounds and odours from all around us. The smell of perfume from the two-masted yacht on our left, the muffled noises and gentle rocking from the blue-hulled motor boat that was different to every other boat movement, the commentary of cricket from yet another. Then I noticed a name on the keel of a boat two walkways over.

'That's his boat, Adam.' I indicated the unassuming green and white cabin cruiser bobbing up and down on the turquoise waves. There was no sign of anyone on board.

'How the hell did you work that out?'

'The clothing outside on the deck is all male. There are bits of ash. and blackened debris all over from some sort of fire, probably a bushfire. And then there's the name.'

'The rest makes sense, Sandie. What about the name, though?'

'*Cherry Ripe*. Barry's pet name for Lauren.'

Quickly we retraced our steps to the shore and made our way along the wooden walkway to Barry's boat.

Adam had left his weapon secured in the police car. When I asked him, he was quick to explain.

'Barry, or Chris when I first met him, wasn't aggressive. Even now, I firmly believe he went on the run to avoid Magnus and the others and not the police. I'm guessing he doesn't know I'm here. The paper didn't mention me by name. Besides, he's probably not aware of that shoot-out the other night.'

'Sounds convincing, Adam. Here was I, thinking you left the gun because it was too hot to wear your shoulder holster and a jacket.'

He grinned. 'Yeah. That too. This Tassie sun is really burning. The extra UV, you say?'

I nodded then we both made our way

closer to Barry's boat. We stepped onto it quietly before I called out.

'Barry. Or Chris. It's Sandie Ashton. Time to come out, mate. We need to talk.'

Nothing happened. Had we missed him yet again? Time was running out on the deadline.

I moved towards the cabin door as it suddenly swung open.

'I'm coming, Sandie. No need for any aggro.' Barry's face, minus beard and moustache, appeared as he emerged, hands held high. 'I see you've brought my old military buddy, Adam. Are you still army, Captain?'

'No, Chris. Federal Police these days.'

'Damn it, you two,' I said angrily. 'My head is spinning with all these name and rank changes. Chris, then Barry. Superintendent, then Captain. It's like playing musical blinking chairs.'

Barry slowly put down his hands, once Adam had frisked him. Despite the situation, he gave a wry smile.

'For the sake of my sanity from now

on you're Barry. Not Chris. Just Barry. Agreed?' I said.

'Technically he was Chris first — ' Adam began before I frowned at him. 'Er, Barry it is, then.'

Barry nodded.

'Suits me. You haven't changed, Sandie Ashton. Still a bossy pain in the rear end. Still wearing a kookaburra's nest on your head. I pity any bloke you end up fancying — ' I must have reacted in some way because Barry's eyes flicked between Adam and me. He burst out laughing.

'You're kidding me. You and the Captain Goody Two Shoes? I simply don't believe that.'

I heard running feet on the wooden slats of the walkway. Jill and Mick.

Mick reached us first. 'Chris Davidson. I'm arresting you for identity — '

'We've agreed to call me Barry, Sergeant. The lovebirds here figured it was easier. And can you arrest me somewhere on land please? I was lying down earlier but standing up, I can feel

my sea-sickness coming back.'

We all regarded the calm waters around us with only a gentle swell. Barry shrugged.

'What can I say? Buying a boat seemed like a good idea once but the last few days hiding out here . . . well, you don't want to go below decks. Trust me. Far too many Technicolor yawns.'

Mick offered a solution. Interrogating him in the cabin had suddenly lost its appeal.

'Grab the knife first, Barry. Magnus has stepped up the stakes for us all. It's bad news.'

'That knife. Wish I'd never stole her. She's under the cabin floor. Anyone want to accompany me?' Considering what we might find inside, we all declined rather quickly.

Barry returned in minutes clutching a Happy Meal cardboard box to his chest. Typical Barry to hide a priceless medieval relic in something like that. It was only as the five of us made our way back to the departure terminal that I

realised that Barry had actually called the knife 'her'.

Walking alongside him, I couldn't understand why. At that point there was some distant voice, speaking in some strange language. Was I imagining it? Was there some radio on? Were the others listening to her?

Then, as we reached the entrance door to the vast building, I heard her again, much closer.

'What's up, Sandie?' Adam asked, concerned.

'Did you notice a woman's voice, close by?'

'Just tourists. No one special or near to us. What did she say?'

'You must have heard. It was soft, yet clear as anything.'

''Fraid not.' He stopped, holding me at arm's length. I paused. I'd already had one fit of madness today. Should I confess to another?

'Sorry. I must be imagining things,' I decided to say. Voices in my head? What next?

14

It must have appeared somewhat bizarre, five people parading through the ferry terminal. Apart from the two uniformed police, the rest of us could have been victims of a crime, witnesses or actual criminals.

Mick led us into a large room with chairs scattered around the sides. Then he disappeared to order a selection of food and drinks. Mick did like his snacks. Nevertheless, we did need to be fully alert.

'Grab yourselves chairs and make a circle. We won't be disturbed,' he announced on his return.

Barry was extremely subdued, the situation having been outlined to him as we had walked from his boat.

'I never meant for any of this to happen, especially involving Lauren and Paula's gran. Sorry, your gran too,

Sandie.' He put the Happy Meal box on the floor in front of all of us. 'That damned knife,' he said angrily.

'Barry. Are you certain it's the knife Magnus wants, and not revenge on you?' Mick asked.

It seemed Barry was willing to co-operate in any way he could. As we had over seven hours until the deadline, we'd agreed to have full disclosure before formulating a plan of action.

'Most definitely,' he said now. 'You all know what that knife is, don't you?'

I decided to play dumb. 'I don't. All I'm aware of is that it's ancient and you stole it in the Middle East while you were in the Army.'

'Me and the others … I gather you've met the two of them already? Yeah, me and the others stole stuff for Magnus. He smuggled it back to Oz or sold it straight to other so-called collectors. You would not believe how well connected he is. Informants everywhere. And before you ask, Adam, I've never seen him or even spoken to

him. Very secretive to the point of paranoia.'

Barry bent down to retrieve the battered box. Opening it, he unwrapped a cloth and held the item out for us all to see.

'Doesn't look much, does she?' he said. It was less than fifteen centimetres long, a dull, grey blade in a slightly more elaborate hilt which was carved symbols all around it. 'Carnwennan. Belonged to Arthur Pendragon, apparently.'

'King Arthur?' Mick exclaimed. 'I thought he was a fairy story, along with Excalibur and all that round table malarkey.'

'Yeah, so did I — before I found her.'

'Barry. You've called the knife 'her' before,' Jill reminded us. 'Any reason for that?'

Barry seemed reluctant to answer at first but eventually sighed and continued. 'She . . . the knife . . . she sort of talks to me sometimes, usually in my dreams. And I'm not going fruit loopy,

although no one else hears her — just me.

'She convinced me not to give her to Magnus. Instead I was to bring her to Tasmania. I swapped identities with the real Barry Denvers, leaving everyone thinking it was Chris who died in that explosion. I became Barry, then I met Paula, and the rest you know.'

Adam was sceptical.

'I thought that the knife was destroyed with you, Chris. It was a surprise to find you alive. As for your 'talking knife', all I'm aware of is that our Government want it desperately. I don't have the full story. The PM explained that it is an object of power — whatever that means.'

Mick asked, 'Barry. Not that I believe you, however does this knife still . . . speak to you?'

'No. Not since I met Paula. The knife brought us together. I showed Carn-wennan to her years ago in the expectation that there was a reason behind us meeting and marrying. The

250

knife glowed a little then returned to its usual appearance. The wacky thing hasn't said a bloody word since.'

Until she spoke to me just now? I wondered.

It was my turn to examine King Arthur's weapon as it was passed around. The instant I touched her, I felt a connection. My mind was awash with images, smells and sounds from people in my past. I saw Mum, much younger, then my gran as a child. It seemed that I was going back in time, glimpsing my ancestral line. Somehow the knife was connecting with me — reading my DNA.

'Sandie . . . Sandie . . . Are you OK?' It was Jill's voice. 'You've gone all pale again.'

I shook my head, feeling as though I was coming out of a hypnotic trance.

'Sorry,' I apologised. 'Low blood sugar.' I picked up two biscuits. The others relaxed and continued talking while I tried to process what had just happened. The flashbacks had stopped

with the vision of a youth standing by a stone holding a sword.

I interrupted their debate.

'This knife isn't metal, by the way. She's a non-brittle ceramic made from boron carbide, aluminium oxide and . . . Doesn't matter. She's virtually indestructible.' I could sense so much about the knife, for some reason.

I passed Carnwennan onto Mick, only then realising that everyone was staring at me.

'What? I did chemistry at school. How else would I know?' I tried to bluff my way out.

Adam nodded. 'If it — sorry, 'she' — is non-metallic that helps explain how she could be smuggled through customs.'

The knife was now being accepted as female by the group. Stranger and stranger.

As Barry put the artefact back into the box, our focus changed to the dire predicament we needed to resolve; saving my family. Adam stood up, moving to the window again. The ferry from Bruny

Island was approaching the dock. He checked his watch.

'Enough about Carnwennan. We need a plan of what to do next.'

I made a suggestion. I guess a part of my somewhat scrambled brain had been planning a way forward ever since we found Barry.

'Magnus doesn't realise we've found Barry. Could I suggest a delaying tactic? How about you contacting his henchmen on that special hotline phone of theirs? Tell them Barry heard the appeal. He's in . . . say . . . Launceston and we're flying him down here. Find out where they want us to take him and the artefact to do the exchange. That will give us more planning time, especially if we have an address for the changeover.'

Adam agreed with that proposal, as did the others. He went into another room to contact Luigi and friend. His intention was to insist on proof that Gran and Lauren were unharmed before any further arrangements were made.

Within minutes he'd returned with an address for the changeover. Adam explained that apparently the captives were not located there so any attempt to rescue them would fail.

'Make sure no coppers are anywhere nearby too,' were the words Luigi had apparently given.

Mick was immediately onto Hobart headquarters, requesting as much information about the rendezvous locality as possible. The building manageress brought us a fax machine which she connected. Within fifteen minutes we had a plan of the beachfront locality south of where we were. It was quite isolated. Moreover we had details of occupants, plus telephone numbers from the electoral rolls and White Pages.

From all appearances, Luigi and Mad Dog had taken over a holiday home not far from a jetty at Verona Sands. From there, they could leave by boat directly into the Tasman Sea. I had

no doubt that, despite our state being an island, the two henchmen could somehow disappear. Magnus appeared to have connections to achieve the impossible. We had their photos everywhere, especially at points where they could leave the island . . . yet that might not be enough.

I offered some more advice.

'What we must do is out-think Magnus's thugs. They'll be there by themselves, I'm sure. Magnus wouldn't take the chance of being caught or seen. We need a distraction, someone getting there before Barry and blending into the surroundings. Mick. You're a man. What would distract you?'

Mick stole a glance at Jill. 'Er . . . a pretty girl, I guess. Maybe in a bikini? But where will we find one of those — a pretty girl, I mean?'

I glared at him. Jill went one better and gave him an angry punch on his shoulder. He realised his error and stammered an apology. Too late.

'You've never seen me in a bikini,

Sergeant Nolan. I could distract any man if I wanted to. Even you.' Jill was pouting. 'Trouble is, I don't have one with me.'

The Sarge was quick to react.

'Absolutely no way, Jill. I can't put you in harm's way. You're too — '

'I'm a policewoman. I'm wearing a police uniform. Or would you prefer that I wasn't?'

Sergeant Nolan blushed a deep shade of scarlet turning his eyes away from Jill.

'Whoops, that came out wrong, didn't it? The point is, I'm willing to go undercover. Perhaps as a 'friend' of one of the locals. Sunbathing in a bikini will be a distraction for Luigi and Mad Dog. I'll keep my distance. I need to get into position quickly — well before you bring Barry and the knife for the exchange.'

Adam nodded in agreement. Eventually Mick did too, despite his protective reservations. He pointed to a house opposite the exchange point. 'This one

has a single woman living there. I'll ring her and set up the deception. When Jill arrives, the owner can come out to greet her like an old friend. Then Jill can change and do some sunbathing on the front lawn of the beach house.'

'I'll go and buy a bikini and some casual clothes. And a beach bag. I'll take some gear from the boot of the police car, just in case. Are these clothes counted as expenses, Sarge?'

'I suppose. Make certain you get receipts. And don't call me Sarge.'

After Jill left, I went over to talk to him.

'Mick. She won't do anything reckless. However we need someone there monitoring the situation. Luigi had demanded that Adam and I accompany Barry with the knife. He'll take our weapons and phones, probably restrain us with our own handcuffs. With Jill keeping you informed while lying there in full sight, we have a chance.'

He nodded. 'That point you made about the handcuffs . . . I thought the

same. I have three sets of special ones being sent from Hobart in an unmarked car for you to use. Trick ones that look real but have a hidden release button. Jill can take the car to Verona Sands. It might give the game away if she arrives in a police vehicle.'

*   *   *

Jill returned ten minutes later, at the same time as the gimmicked handcuffs. She looked every bit the sunbathing beauty. Her chestnut hair fell across her shoulders, the straw hat and gaudy sunnies complementing the bright multi-coloured sarong and green sandals with a matching oversized beach bag. It was perfect as a disguise.

'Now for my cossie,' she announced taking off the hat and glasses. She undid the knot of the sarong and let it fall to the carpet, posing with one hand on a hip and one knee bent slightly.

The three men gasped. Even I was impressed . . . and a little jealous. I

could never be brave enough to wear such a skimpy bikini. It made a mockery of the term 'undercover officer'.

'Constable Isherwood . . . Jill . . . I . . .' Mick began.

'Am I a big enough distraction, Sergeant? Adam?' Jill asked innocently.

Adam cleared his throat, obviously also stunned.

'Shall I turn around?' Jill asked as she did so.

Mick tried to say 'No,' but was too slow. I realised that he, Barry and Adam couldn't help themselves, being men and all. However I did object to Adam's more than professional interest. As for Jill's bikini . . .

I spoke up. 'All right, Jill. You've made your point. Get dressed again, please. Adam, I think you've seen enough of our young constable. We need to talk.'

Mick stayed with Jill. I heard her give him the receipts for expenses.

'This can't be right, Constable. That bikini? Two hundred and twenty dollars?' he cried out.

'I know. It was fortunate I found one in the sale that was my size,' Jill responded.

Mick said a few naughty words at that point. Their voices became quieter after that as they went over procedures and checked the items in her beach bag.

In the meantime Barry, Adam and I made our own plans. The aim was first and foremost to ensure the safety of Lauren and my gran. Keeping control of the knife and capturing Magnus was next. Saving the three of us from ending up dead at the hands of Luigi and Mad Dog . . . well, that was up to Jill and her bikini. I prayed they'd both be up to the task.

Jill was ready to leave. We double-checked our plans and the anticipated actions of the kidnappers.

'You be careful, Constable Isherwood,' Mick said at the door. We couldn't take the chance of her being seen outside with us.

'Of course, Sergeant. I'll have SPF50

sun screen on. Don't want to get burned, do I?' Jill returned cheekily.

★ ★ ★

It was five thirty-five; twenty minutes' drive to the beach. We planned to arrive forty minutes later, time enough for Jill to make herself at home across the road and set the trap for the criminals.

As we awaited our turn to leave, Adam elected to ring Luigi, pretending that Barry had arrived by flight from Launceston.

I contacted my sister at the hospital, both to update her on the situation and to enquire about Grandad. He was doing fine.

Mick was contacting his superiors to be ready to deploy when needed. Barry remained in the room, deep in his own thoughts. Carnwennan was at his side. It seemed bizarre that such a valuable piece of history was kept in a child's food box. I wondered how Ronald McDonald would fit in, seated at the

Round Table with Arthur, Lancelot and the others.

Was I imagining that voice in my head? I wasn't certain. All I understood was that the next few hours were crucial for us all, and I had a job to do.

Adam came up to hold me and kiss my head from behind. I turned to give him a proper one in return.

'Good grief,' said Barry. 'Is that professional?'

'Shut up, Barry,' Adam and I told him together. Maybe it was the dangerous situation we were facing or possibly it was simply the need for someone to love after all I'd been through in the past month. I couldn't think about how our relationship could continue when we returned to our respective headquarters. That long-distance thing would be a big problem.

★ ★ ★

We drove down in Barry's car. It was early Friday evening so the Channel

Highway wasn't too busy. The picturesque drive south along the Derwent River was spectacular.

Barry made a comment about boats and his sea-sickness. 'I'm selling Cherry Ripe as soon as this is all over. Provided I'm still alive. If I ever see another boat in my lifetime, it'll be too soon.'

'I wouldn't worry, mate. Assuming we make it out of this in one piece, you're off to jail. Smuggling, identity theft, putting a priceless medieval knife in a box that stinks of hamburgers.'

'Yeah. I realise that. At least Lauren will be OK. I love her. She's the only decent thing I've done with my life.'

★ ★ ★

When we arrived in the street for the rendezvous, we all tried to ignore Jill sunning herself on a lounger. Even though it was late afternoon, it was hot and sunny. She was sitting up, opposite the criminal's lair, applying her sunscreen. There was a For Sale sign outside.

Before we got out, I had a change of heart. For Adam and Barry to totally ignore her was too implausible. After all, they were men.

'OK, you can look — but just enough to make it believable. Remember why we're here. And bring your Happy Meal box, Barry.'

There was a car parked on the drive of Lover's Retreat, the name of the house that Luigi and Mad Dog had broken into. They'd probably done some research on the real owner so that they could pretend to be there with permission if any nosy neighbour asked.

Behind us, I heard Jill chatting with the woman living opposite, talking about having a barbie later. It was all going according to plan.

Luigi opened the door before we knocked. He must have been awaiting us. Or, more likely, he and Mad Dog had been ogling Jill across the road. That bikini appeared to be having the desired effect. Mad Dog came to the door. He waved to Jill, who waved back.

'Get inside, you three,' Luigi whispered, menacingly. Even before he'd closed the door, he had a knife to Barry's throat. 'You've led us a merry chase over the years, Chris.'

'He's called Barry now,' I said, hoping to avoid another headache with this Chris/Barry confusion.

'Barry then, you stupid sheila. Drag yourself away from that door, MD. Take their phones and any weapons.'

Mad Dog lumbered over, doing as he was told. When it came to my turn, I offered to put everything out of my pockets rather than let him put his grubby hands on me. Unfortunately, he frisked me anyway.

'Looky here, Luigi. Handycuffs. We can use them to lock these galahs up. Never was much good at tying knots meself.'

'They're called 'handcuffs', you pelican. But it's a good idea. Do it. Hands behind their backs. And give us the knife.'

'Hold on,' said Barry. 'What about

the deal? You let Lauren and the old lady go.'

'It's not up to me. I take the special souvenir to the big boss and he decides. He doesn't want the rug-rat or the wrinkly; only the knife.'

'He gets the knife, then we all can go home?' Adam asked, just as our hands were cuffed to three of the dining chairs pushed up against a wall.

Luigi paused before walking up to gloat at us. He fingered the gun in his hand.

'Not quite. The kid and the old woman go home. However regarding the three of you — ' He bent over to stare at us, face to face. 'We're going to kill you . . . one by one.'

15

Kill us? I felt sick. My bad hair day was going from bad to blinking disastrous.

'Come on,' said Adam. 'We've done everything you guys wanted. We found Barry. We've come here with the artefact. At least let the girl go.'

Barry said nothing. He was staring blankly at the table in front of him. I suspected that he was resigned to dying for having put his daughter in danger. I wasn't as ready to give up.

Luigi poked his grubby finger at me.

'Girl? She's a woman. Plus she's the reason our mate got caught.' Luigi wasn't changing his mind, it seemed. 'Naw. I'm going to shoot her but I'll do her last of all. She can watch as I do Chris or Barry or whatever, then this bloke who locked us up for years, then you, missy. We might take our time with you though. Not many sheilas in jail,

were there, MD? . . . MD?'

'I think he's too busy looking through the window, Luigi.' Adam nodded towards Mad Dog. It seemed like Jill's diversion was working on at least one of the two thugs.

Luigi burst out laughing. 'You actually believed me when I said we'd kill you? It was a joke. You idiots are so dense. We don't need to do that. In fact, you done us a favour by putting the other guy in jail.'

I was somewhat relieved to hear we were not going to die after all. Needless to say, I wasn't that impressed by Luigi's idea of a joke.

'Did you a favour? How?'

'With him out of the way, we don't have to split all the money our boss is giving us into three,' the shorter member of the gang explained.

'Yeah, you stupid sheila. Now we get half each.' Mad Dog was close to my face as he explained. He had some serious dental hygiene issues as well as not having seen a bar of soap for some

weeks. He appeared to lose interest at that point. 'Can I go now, Luigi? Thinking 'bout numbers hurts my brain.' He went back to the window. 'That pretty girlie; she's moving around again, Luigi. Seems like she's making a barbie. And she's still wearing that bikkie thing.'

'He means 'bikini',' Luigi explained to the three of us, seemingly glad to have someone sensible to talk to for a change, even if we were the enemy. 'MD. I want you to take the knife to the Boss. You know where to go, don't you? Then he can release the old lady and the kid and we can all get off this dump of an island.'

'Right, Luigi. I'll take the knife and drive, then come back here for you.' Mad Dog picked up the car keys and was about to open the front door to the weatherboard house when Luigi shouted.

'You forgot the knife, you pelican.'

'Yeah. 'Spose it would help if I took it. Be right back.'

It was a slip of the tongue yet it told Adam and me that wherever he was

going was close.

I imagined that the paranoid desire of Magnus to keep his identity secret, even from his trusted henchmen, would mean that Mad Dog would drop the knife off somewhere, drive off, then Magnus would come out of his surveillance location to retrieve Carnwennan. Once that was done, Magnus would release my family or at least tell the police where they were. Catching Magnus and retrieving the knife would be the ideal end result.

That was the plan.

But what did that Scots bloke, Robert Burns, say in his poem, *To a Mouse? The best laid schemes o' mice an' men Gang aft a-gley.* My Scottish wasn't all that bright but 'gang aft a-gley' sounded awfully like the Aussie expression, 'can get totally mucked up'.

If only Magnus didn't find the minuscule radio-trackers in the cloth wrapping around Carnwennan.

★ ★ ★

While we waited patiently for Mad Dog to return, I had a good squizz at Luigi and our surroundings. We could have all broken out of the trick handcuffs at any time. There wasn't any point now though, not until we had confirmation that Gran and little Lauren were safe and sound.

Luigi was the brighter of our two captors. That was obvious. Even so, he spent a lot of time spying on Jill across the road. What was it Gran used to say? *Men have a one-track mind and that's covered in dirt.*

She wasn't wrong. Jill was the ultimate misdirection. It was such a shame that she had to belittle herself in this way, though.

I guessed Luigi and his hulking partner in crime had been staying here since the shearing shed. There were half-eaten take-aways, bits of food and empty tinnies scattered everywhere in the open plan kitchen and family room. Full ash trays and a packet of cigarettes lay on the table. A broken glass pane in

271

the back door revealed how they'd broken in. I shuddered to think what state the bedrooms and bathroom would be in.

Before we could achieve much, Luigi proclaimed that Mad Dog was back. As I thought, the drop-off point must have been less than five k away from where we were. Luigi's mobile phone rang. He spoke a little, though it was mainly listening. Finally he turned to us just as his fellow kidnapper re-entered the building.

'That was the boss. He told me that because you brought him the knife thingy, he's releasing the prisoners.'

I was relieved, as I imagined, Adam and Barry were. 'What proof do we have?' I asked.

'He said that it should be on the news soon. Oh yeah, he wasn't very happy to find two radio-bugs with the knife.'

Damn. So much for that plan.

'You cops reckon you're so smart, don't you? Our boss is loads smarter though. Makes you all look like a bunch of dipsy drongos. Guess where they are?

Tied up in a van outside the main police station in Hobart.'

Minutes later, there was a news bulletin on the telly which confirmed that. It seemed the reporter had been tipped off to be there with a cameraman. The release of the victims was live. They both appeared to be tied, gagged but unharmed. Thank goodness. We could break free now — except for our captors. If only they weren't so cautious.

I wasn't bothered that finding my family in that location would be embarrassing for the police. This Magnus was one brazen criminal, showing off like that. The van had been parked there for hours. It had two parking tickets — yet no one had realised my family were trapped inside.

'How is it going to work from now, Luigi? Your boss has what he wants. He's won. Probably leaving Tasmania as we speak because no one has any idea what he looks like. Yeah, he's dead clever. Much cleverer than us drongo

273

cops . . . as well as you.'

'Us? What are you talking about? We're going to be rich, and when we leave this stinking backward dump we'll . . .'

'Have your mug-shots on the notice boards of every police station in Australia? New Zealand? Maybe the whole world? You'll be on the run forever.' I let that sink in.

'What's she talking about, Luigi? I don't wanna be hunted down.' MD was listening, his spying on Jill temporally forgotten.

'Let me guess. You leave us in handcuffs, take that fast boat moored at the pier then meet up with a tramp steamer just outside the twenty kay territorial limit?'

'How did she know that, Luigi?'

'Shut up, you stupid pelican. She's guessing.'

I wasn't finished. Luigi was well back from us, waving his pistol around. There was no chance of getting the jump on him, even though I was positive that

Adam had released his cuffs just as I had.

'You realise what your clever boss has done, don't you? Told you there'll be a ship to pick you up to escape. Only thing is, what happens when it's not there? You either try to get to a safe country by yourselves on a little motor boat or you end up swimming there.'

'Luigi. What if she's right? He don't need us no more. He said so. I can't swim.'

'Shut up, you moron. Shut up. Shut up.' Luigi glared at me. He was breathing heavily.

'You. You are one clever bitch, lady. You're trying to scare us. Make us do something we'll regret. I don't believe your evil lies. The boss wouldn't let us down. That ship will be there to pick us up. But you . . . none of you will be alive to find out. You're all gong to be dead.'

Barry didn't budge. He was staring at the floor. Adam spoke up though.

'Come off it, Luigi. You tried that

'I'm going to kill you speech' before,
Then you said it was a joke remember?'

Luigi levelled his gun at us, menacingly. 'MD. Drag yourself away from the bloody window.'

'But she's doing the barbie.'

'Do as I say, MD. Start pouring those petrol cans from the other room all over. We're going to have our own barbeque.'

'We are?' MD clapped his hands. 'What are we having?'

Luigi bared his teeth at us. 'Roast pig.'

Things were looking real bad. I began to sweat.

Adam yelled out. 'At least let her go.'

'No chance, copper. You's all going to die. Just like I said before.'

MD was finished with one petrol container. He was sloshing the other can over the kitchen worktop and settees. The fumes were getting on my chest. The smell was almost overpowering.

There was a loud knock at the front door. Both men froze. Luigi hushed us.

'Anyone says one word and I kill you

276

and them too. MD, see who it is.'

The huge henchman put down the petrol can, wiped his hands on his grubby checked shirt and peeked out from behind a velvet curtain.

'It's that pretty sheila.'

'Get rid of her.'

MD opened the door but, due to our position, we were unable to see outside. There was a muffled conversation then MD turned to Luigi. 'She's inviting us all to her barbie. Can we go?' He was frothing at the mouth quite profusely.

'No. Of course we can't go. Tell her . . . tell her we've already started our own dinner.'

I could hear Jill more clearly now. 'What are you having? Perhaps we could share it together.'

'No, sorry, pretty girlie. We can't come. I like your bikki though.'

I decided that was it. Our deception had failed. Luigi had kept us under watch the whole time and his finger was poised on the trigger. MD reluctantly said goodbye, but kept the door ajar.

Presumably he wanted one final look as Jill began to walk back to the other home. I could just see her waving her arms around in a strange fashion.

Adam must have realised that we were on our own. I felt him tense to jump Luigi while MD's back was turned. It was suicide, and he realised it — but it would give me a fighting chance.

This was it; our last option.

'Ready?' he whispered to me just as Luigi turned slightly.

16

'No. Wait,' I replied. Adam stared at me angrily. The moment of opportunity had passed.

'Shut up, you two.' Luigi backed up to finish with the petrol can. He kicked it over, still watching the three of us. 'MD. Close the door.'

MD ignored him. He shouted to Jill. 'Why ya waving your hands like that?'

I could see through the net curtain that she'd stopped and was walking back towards him.

'Mozzies. They keep biting me. Actually you could help me, please? I have some insect repellent spray here.'

Luigi was backing up towards the front door, still watching us carefully. He wasn't happy.

'Get back inside, MD.'

MD didn't seem to hear him. Or, if he did, helping Jill was more important

279

than following Luigi's instructions.

'Yeah, sure. I'll spray you, missy. All over.' I could just perceive that Jill was at the door again right in front of MD. 'Give me the mozzy spray, please,' he said.

'Certainly,' she replied. A moment passed then there came the sound of an aerosol spray.

'Aaaaagh!' Mad Dog screamed. 'My eyes — ' He stumbled backwards into the shack, hitting Luigi, who dropped his gun as he fell over.

'Adam. Now. You take MD. I'll handle this one.'

Luigi was quick. He scrambled to regain his footing, grabbing for his gun. I was quicker, kicking the weapon out of reach. The distinctive odour of pepper spray mingled with the smell of petrol. No wonder MD was in agony.

My hands and legs were stiff from inactivity so I was slower than I should have been. Luigi was manic, sliding and slipping on the fuel-covered tiles. He wasn't giving up without one hell of a battle.

Adam and MD were fighting outside. Again, despite a face full of pepper spray, the huge thug was lashing out viciously. I noticed Adam go down from a lucky blow by MD.

'Jill. I'll sort this. Secure the weapons. Check on Barry. Then get out. This place is a tinder box.'

Luigi made another dash for his gun. He shoved me, pushing me off balance to smash into the camping stove fitted into the worktop. I was panting from the exertion as well as the pungent smells.

'Damn you, Luigi. Stay down,' I yelled, bringing him down with a kick to the back of one knee. 'Jill. Get his gun. I can't stop him much longer.'

Jill gathered the gun from the floor into a shopping bag, along with the others.

Meanwhile I'd slipped, landing on the Italian's back. It knocked the breath from him. Regaining control, I kept my knee pressed his back as he fought and squirmed. Once, twice, he almost managed to push me off. It was like riding one of those bucking broncos in some

amusement arcades, except this one called me every filthy word in the book.

'Enough!' I shouted and held his face to the floor. Every part of my body ached. I just prayed that my left arm was still in one piece. 'Jill. Some rope, clothes line. Anything.'

She cut some cord off the Venetians with a knife from the shopping bag and tossed it. Thank goodness. My strength was almost gone. I held him down as Jill tied his wrists.

'Get Barry. He's not moving. Might be in shock? Get yourselves out of here.'

I forced Luigi to his feet. He appeared more passive now, thank goodness. I was about to force him outside when Jill called out that she couldn't release Barry from the chair. The trick handcuffs had stuck.

'On your knees, Luigi.' He complied grudgingly. I knew how difficult it was to balance and stand with your hands bound behind your back. Then I went over to Barry. 'Get out, Jill. Take the guns.'

Jill ran outside. I could still hear Adam and MD slugging it out on the front decking.

Finally I managed to free Barry's hands. He was so groggy. I couldn't understand why. I pushed him towards the front door just as I noticed that Luigi had moved. Somehow he was in front of the stove. The hiss of escaping gas told me all I needed to know. Even with his hands bound, he wasn't giving up.

'Die, you bastard copper,' he snarled. He turned his back to the stove to fumble around for the piezo-electric ignition button with his tied hands. Gas and petrol fumes? Not a good combination when there's a spark. Panic time.

'Move yourself, Barry. Now,' I screamed, hoping it might register in his addled brain.

Fortunately my ex-brother-in-law seemed to realise what was happening. He pushed me in front of him just as the house exploded in one humungous fireball. Luigi wouldn't have stood a chance — but we

were literally blown out through the open door, over the wooden decked veranda and onto the lush grass in the front.

* * *

Barry lay sprawled at my side, having borne the full brunt of the detonation. The back of his shirt was alight. Before I could struggle to my feet, the lady from across the road was there, ripping the burning clothing from his body.

'You all right, love?' she asked me.

'Yeah . . . Ears are ringing but OK, thanks.' I bent down to examine Barry's back. He was groggy. Thankfully, the flames from his shirt hadn't got through his singlet.

'Fireys, ambos and cops?' I asked the heroic woman.

She held up her mobile. 'On their way.' She pointed to the blazing ruin of the beach-side retreat. 'Poor Mr Tomkin's house. What happened?'

'Petrol, bottled gas . . . you name it.'

Then I noticed Adam pushing MD

towards us, his hands enclosed in proper cuffs from Jill's shopping bag. They both seemed unharmed by the devastating blast. Burning debris was scattered everywhere with flames still licking the charred timbers of the collapsed roof.

'Luigi?' he asked.

'Must be dead. He was at the centre of it all. Where's Jill?'

'Getting some clothes on, I hope.'

'It worked, though. She and that bikini saved our lives.'

'She also helped me subdue Mad Dog. The guy's built like a wrestler, plus I'm not that young any more. I was just about to collapse when Jill came out of the house, saw that I was in trouble and stood up to Mad Dog herself. She's so fragile looking but today I saw a different side of her — and I'm not referring to her state of undress.'

I was intrigued. 'What did she do?'

'Faced up to him. Fifty kilos to his one thirty. From where I was lying, I

reckoned she was a goner. She kicked him you know where, yelled out 'Pervert', then whacked his head with her shopping bag. It was like Darlene and Goliath. He went down like a sack of spuds.'

'Shopping bag? The one with the guns in it? No wonder he went down.' *Poor MD*, I thought.

Sirens began to be heard as the other residents of the road came out to view what had occurred. Some ran forward to assist us all to safety.

Jill appeared from the other side of the street, wearing her sarong. She dashed over, arriving just as the volunteer fire brigade appliances turned into the dirt road.

'Glad you're OK, Sandie. All of you.'

'Not quite all,' I commented, sadly. 'Luigi's dead. Why did he do what he did?'

It was a rhetorical question to no one in particular, so it was a surprise when Barry piped up in reply.

'He's a pyro. Always loved fires. I

guess he was so fascinated with setting them, he couldn't bear the thought of missing out on one last inferno.'

'You're OK, then? You seemed so out of it, inside,' I said, hugging him. 'You saved my life. Thank you.'

'You saved mine first. Back there. I just couldn't think, except about how I'd almost ruined so many lives. Even yours. You've never liked me and I can understand why. I kept kidding myself I was a good person, yet you saw the real me. That's what happened in there. I saw the real me for the first time and I didn't like him at all. Chris . . . Barry . . . neither of them was worth saving. But you did — you helped me escape.'

We began to congregate around the ambulances. Mick pulled up at the same time.

Adam was the first to ask.

'Did we catch him? Magnus?'

Mick shook his head. 'Unfortunately not. Despite all the things we tried — the hidden transmitters, the checkpoints — he's outsmarted us once

more. He's like a ghost.

'The only consolation we have is that the girl and Sandie's gran are both fine. We'll do a quick debrief now before we take Barry and that huge Mad Dog guy to prison. Your sister is staying with Lauren at your grandparents' place tonight. She wants you there too, unless you need to go to hospital. Adam can drive you, if that's OK.'

I nodded before taking Jill to one side for a quiet word.

'Adam described how you bashed Mad Dog with a shopping bag full of guns and phones. Why not use one of the guns as it was intended to be used?'

Jill grinned. 'A well-respected friend of mine called Sandie once asked if I could shoot a person and I told her I didn't know. That's why I chose to kabong him with the guns instead. Eminently more satisfying.'

In some bizarre way her logic made sense. I decided that Jill was Jill, and to leave it at that.

It was about eight o'clock at night. Almost dusk. I left Adam and Jill to continue the debrief. I'd just noticed something I wanted to check out. It was personal.

I wandered across the very crowded street to the house where Jill had been sunbathing. The owner was sitting on a chair.

Barry was being checked over by one ambo team while MD had another, with two burly police standing by him. Just another peaceful evening in Verona Sands.

'G'day. I'm Sandie. I'm related to the kidnap victims.'

'Anne. Pleased to meet you. Jill told me who you are. Have a seat, and a cuppa if you want.' She was in her late forties, dressed in a loose-fitting cotton frock and sandals.

'Actually I'd prefer something cold after that close call. Got a cider?'

'Yeah, sure.' She opened the Esky

cool box at her side. I thanked her as I pulled the tab.

'I wanted to ask you a question or two. I see you have your house up for sale with Mandeville. Did you ever approach Paula Ashton up in Hobart to sell it?'

'Matter of fact, I did. Lovely lady. Would have preferred to deal with her but it didn't happen.'

I sat forward on my chair, taking a long blissful swig from the ice-cold tinnie.

'Oh. I'm sorry to hear that, Anne. Mind telling me why?'

★ ★ ★

The night-time drive to Huonville was one of those quiet times for us both. I imagined Adam was angry he'd lost the knife as well as dealing with the shock of the horrendous fight and explosion. Having a person, even a vicious criminal like Luigi, die on his op must have taken its toll.

290

It was late when we arrived. There was an emotional reunion for my family with lots of tears and cuddles. None of us had been seriously injured, though I suspected the mental scars would be with us for some time. I could imagine Lauren having nightmares.

Unlike the aftermath of Darling Harbour, I felt strong. I was positive about what I wished to do with my life, and being a cop was exactly it. Today I'd achieved something to be proud of.

Also there was Adam; dear, brave, sweet Adam. He'd come into my life as a Mystery Man and, no doubt would soon leave it again to return to Canberra while I went back to Sydney. I wondered how long we might have together and if our long-distance relationship would work. He'd informed me that he could spend some time in the Sydney office of the Feds, but even so . . .

Grandad seemed perkier than before. Maybe it was the meds. In any case he made us a late dinner, insisting we both needed looking after.

Gran was the one who suggested Adam could stay for the night.

'We have an extra bedroom if you want. It'll save that long drive back to your hotel, young man. Of course it's up to you — though I reckon you've had a long day already.'

'That's very kind of you, Mrs Avalon. If it's no trouble I'll take you up on that offer.'

'You can sleep in the old wing of the house. There's only the one bedroom so you won't be disturbed. You have your own bathroom down there, Adam.'

'But that's my — ' I began.

'Can you help me with the sheets, Sandie?'

I was fuming. 'Where will I sleep?' I asked once we were out of earshot.

'Wherever you want, Sandie. You could bunk in with Paula or . . . damn it, girl. Do I have to do everything for you? You both fancy one another and I haven't time to argue. I learned something important today. Seize the moment. Your choice.'

She pulled sheets and pillowcases from the hall wardrobe and dumped them in my arms. We made our way back to the others where I stood holding the bedclothes. I glanced at Adam, then Gran before returning my gaze to him.

'Come with me, Adam. I'll show you to your room . . . It has a double bed.'

17

When we arrived at the breakfast table on Saturday morning, the others were already there.

'Did you sleep well?' Paula asked.

'Actually we didn't get much sleep. We were . . . ' I began.

Paula put her hands over Lauren's ears.

'Too much information, little sis.'

I gave her a wry smile before continuing. 'We were . . . talking most of the time.'

'Only most?' Gran said with a wink. I might have blushed a little but was comforted by Adam placing his hand on mine. His touch felt so right.

Throughout our morning meal, Adam kept brushing his hands over my skin or letting me do the same to him. It was like an unspoken language, one I'd never shared with any man before.

If the others noticed they didn't let on, that is, until Lauren asked why we were doing that.

'Are you both itchy?' she decided. 'Mum has some cream for that.'

Paula declared she was going to the office as she'd neglected the business during the past, eventful week. She hoped it was still there.

'Are you coming in, Sandie?' she enquired.

'Yes. I'll go in with Adam. He can drop me off. Then he's off to police headquarters. Lots of paperwork.'

'Will we see you again, Adam?' Grandad asked.

'Not sure yet, Mr Avalon. The criminal mastermind can't be found and neither can the priceless item he stole. It depends if there are any leads as to where he's gone. Alternatively I might take some time off to look around this beautiful state of yours.' He put his arm around my shoulder. 'Perhaps a goodbye might be in order today, though I do want to see you again.'

Paula had been in the office for some time before I arrived. The Witch was showing homes to prospective clients which gave me the opportunity to make some phone calls of my own. We had a new receptionist who'd been recruited to take over Holly's former job. Paula had appointed Holly as a full time sales consultant, steam-rolling over Yvonne's vocal objections that there wasn't enough call for a third saleswoman.

The new receptionist was as warm and engaging as Holly. Hardly surprising, as she was Holly's younger sister.

Stephen was beavering away on the system changeover.

'Sandie. My office. Ask Stephen and Holly to come in, too.'

Paula wasn't in a happy mood. Embezzlement was unthinkable in this close-knit group of women, yet it had happened. Holly had some serious questions to answer.

'Holly. Stephen has discovered quite

a few accounts that have been unpaid until now. Our business finances are much healthier than you, or I, thought on New Year's Eve. Before you say anything, I understand a lot of that was before you took over, and you always wanted the MYOB programme. Nevertheless . . . ' Paula paused before continuing. She was about to accuse a trusted employee of theft, and it was difficult.

Paula produced a number of bank statements plus pages from Holly's own ledgers.

'This account with over thirty-six thousand dollars in it. Who set it up?'

Holly scanned the paperwork, appearing upset.

'I opened it. You told me to. What's going on?'

'I told you to?'

'Yes. You wanted it kept off the grid. I don't know why. Tax avoidance? Not my role to question you, Paula.'

The atmosphere was very icy. A penguin would have been in his element at that moment.

'Wait. I'll get the letter you wrote authorising me to open this account alongside your others.'

Holly scurried off to her filing cabinets while the three of us wondered what was going on. She returned, dumping a thick file on Paula's desk.

'Paula. I've always tried my best. Why are you doing this to me?' She was ready to burst into tears. It clearly wasn't an act.

Paula held up a sheet of paper.

'This isn't my signature. Who gave it to you?'

'Yvonne. It was just after I started doing the job. Are you saying she's forged your authority and signature? I never imagined — '

Paula came around the desk to console her. Stephen and I felt a wave of relief. The only dishonest member of the staff was Yvonne.

It was now time for full disclosure. Holly seemed OK now, though angry she'd been duped by Yvonne. We all were.

Apart from the siphoning off of business monies via the bogus bank account, it seemed Witchy Yvonne had been getting back-handers into the same account from Mandeville's. My own phone calls this morning to previous rental clients as well as those wishing to sell their properties told us that Yvonne had been telling lies, causing Paula's clients to leave her company.

Yesterday's lady at Verona Sands had wanted to advertise with Paula. It was Yvonne who'd told her Paula wouldn't do it, due to the distance. She'd actually suggested Mandeville's, giving Anne a card for Paula's opposition.

Armed with promises from Paula's former clients to provide affidavits about Yvonne's actions and the paper trail of the forgery/bogus account, Paula contacted her Real Estate governing body. She requested suspension of Yvonne's licence as well as a formal investigation of Mandeville's illegal practices.

The president tried to smooth it over

with platitudes and promises of a warning letter. That's when I took over the phone conversation. By the time I'd explained my position as a police officer, he had become much more compliant.

'That'll teach him to mess with my big sister,' I said as I put the receiver down.

The bank account had been frozen by Paula and Stephen with the funds transferred to Paula's working account. Fortunately Yvonne hadn't tried to draw monies from it.

Outside in the open plan office, I could see that Holly and Stephen were engrossed in the new computer spreadsheets. Paula was paying for his services, now that she was quite solvent again.

* * *

Paula surmised that Yvonne had been intent on destroying her business little by little. Once Paula was forced to close, Yvonne probably already had a job lined up with Mandeville's.

Yvonne had no idea we were on to her conniving schemes yet. Although I would have enjoyed being present with the conversation between her and Paula, I had my own work to do.

'Holly. I need a word. How's it going in sales?'

'Great! Sold two properties already. I love it.'

I was so pleased for her.

'I just wanted to check your recollection of that day Paula was taken at Bandicoot Drive. Paula said that the kidnappers were waiting for her when she arrived. What I can't work out is how they could possibly have known she'd be there at that time. Any ideas?'

Holly shook her head. 'I never spoke to Mr Dobbs. You were on the front desk in the morning. Did he ring you?'

Holly was right. He'd rung me with the meeting time and his address. I'd told Paula as she was heading out somewhere. My own memories of that horrendous day were hazy, probably

due to that darned infection from the broken glass.

'Yes. I'd forgotten. I passed the message on to Paula. She was on the way out with that older couple from on my flight.' I was thinking aloud by this time. Holly had never met the East-mans —

Wait. I stood there trying to process the terrifying facts. That Bill character . . . he was Magnus. He must be. That was the only thing that made sense.

Other pieces clicked into place. I mentally kicked myself for being so easily taken in. My boss in Sydney bumping my flight so that I'd be on the same flight as Magnus, whom he'd expected me to recognise through my intuition. That had failed spectacularly. Also Magnus coming from overseas — the passports in Val's handbag . . . If she was his wife, that is.

I had missed all the indications that Bill was this arch-villain. Stupid, stupid me. I dialled Adam.

'Adam. I've worked out who Magnus

is.' I explained about my conclusions.

'That old hen-pecked old guy from the docks? Wow. That is one helluva disguise. Who would have imagined . . . I wonder. If he's so unpredictable, might he still be here in Tasmania? We expected him to make his getaway last night.'

'Try asking the Hobart hotels first and work outwards. Their names were . . . ' I struggled to recall. 'Val and Bill East-man.' I heard Adam giving instructions to other officers in Headquarters, including descriptions as they may have done a Barry and be using aliases. 'I'll ring you back when we locate them. You realise what this means? We could still catch him . . . '

'And retrieve Carnwennan,' I added, feeling a surge of excitement.

*　*　*

Soon afterwards, Adam phoned back. 'They're staying in somewhere called Battery Point, checking out today. They

have a taxi booked for twelve-fifteen, to the airport.'

I checked my watch. Twenty minutes. Not enough time to substitute our driver, therefore a discreet diversion was needed. Although it would be tight, we could be set up to intercept them on the one approach road to the airport before they checked in.

We had the taxi company name. At least we could isolate them, since we had no idea what Magnus or his wife were capable of in a crowd.

There weren't any photos to circulate. Adam and I were the only ones who could pick them out, apart from Paula who had met them at the docks. Moreover, Adam had seen them only for a minute on the plane when we all arrived. There was police back-up on the road and at the terminal, including Mick and Jill.

We waited and waited. Nothing. When Adam contacted the hotel, they told him Bill and Val had not been there for the pick-up.

'They must have booked that taxi as a diversion,' he declared angrily. Once more, we'd been out-manoeuvred by this cunning genius.

'They're probably already in the terminal.' We headed off to the parking area a short drive away. Jill phoned just then, confirming some people, using their names, had checked in and were waiting at the boarding gate surrounded by other waiting passengers. Damn.

Inside we met up with her and Mick. Jill appeared much more professional fully clothed.

'They're in there, for sure. Front right hand side,' I confirmed, peering through a one-way security screen. 'We need to isolate them.'

'Jill was thinking quickly. 'We can bring them to us. An announcement that their hold luggage has split open. Presumably the knife is in there.'

I wasn't convinced. Being ceramic, it wouldn't have set the alarms off in the people scanners.

'They'll be suspicious.'

'But they'll come. It would draw attention if they didn't and Magnus hates to be noticed.'

The announcement was made. The attendant took them to the door leading to the basic baggage loading room. Mick was dressed as a handler. It should have been the perfect ruse yet something gave us away as we hid behind the door they were coming through; a movement, a shadow, the sound of a shoe.

Immediately Bill grabbed the young employee, holding her by her arms as he entered.

'Don't anyone budge or I shoot her!'

How the hell did he bring a gun through security?

'OK. OK,' shouted Adam, lowering his weapon while backing away from him. Bill pushed the door closed. The six of us were alone at least but we hadn't reckoned on a civilian employee being caught up in the drama. I tried to weigh up the options to deal with Magnus without jeopardising the life of

the terrified woman.

It was Mick who acted. He was at one side of the room in his baggage handler disguise. Magnus had been focusing on us. Mick flung their suitcase to the floor, causing Magnus to move. Jill jumped forward, pushing the attendant out of his loose grip around her body. Adam had his gun back up faster than the old man could react.

'Drop it, sport. Or else.' Adam's voice was commanding. Bill did as he was told, letting the pistol clatter to the concrete floor.

We'd done it. Magnus was in custody.

'Face down on the ground.' Magnus fell to his knees while Jill took the sobbing attendant back into the departure lounge. Mick and Adam went to cuff the old man, who had finally been exposed as a master criminal. Having done that, they checked the baggage and Bill's body for the precious artefact.

Yet I had one of my feelings that things weren't right. The knife was not

to be found. If Bill wasn't Magnus, then who . . . ?

I turned just in time to see Val Eastman lift the pistol her husband had dropped and level it at us.

'*She's* Magnus,' I said, stating the now blindingly obvious. We were in trouble. Her gentle countenance was now that of a snarling animal.

'Release my husband, you filthy pig scum,' she barked, vehemently.

Bill scrambled to his feet as his wife herded the three of us up against a wall.

Adam tried desperately to reason with Val.

'There's no way out. The police will know who you are, Magnus. Your anonymity is gone. Give yourself up.'

Magnus took aim, her face contorted in rage.

'No. I still have some tricks. I can disappear again. However you coppers will pay for what you've done to me. Pay dearly. Call it revenge. Call it an old woman's loss of objectivity. Call it my idea of fun. It really doesn't matter.

You've destroyed my plans for the final time. Now die.'

This time there was no choice. The three of us dived forward, praying that we could stop her even if she shot one of us.

But no shots were fired. Instead there was a deafening scream as Val doubled up in pain.

'My leg!' she yelled, dropping the gun as she writhed in agony. The men restrained her as I retrieved her weapon. She scrambled at her boot, shrieking in pain until she unzipped it. The knife fell to the floor, still glowing red. Val's leg was badly burned but I, for one, didn't care.

Tears streamed down her face. I watched the knife cool until I could pick her up in safety.

★　★　★

Sunday was an unusual day for Adam and me. The entire drama involving Barry and Magnus was complete. The

consequences, however, were not.

Adam and I had spent some time speculating about the ancient knife of King Arthur. Like Excalibur, Carnwennan appeared to be a conduit to eldritch power. She'd acted to protect me in some mystic way. Me, a descendant of her once master, the Arthur of legends.

Adam further suggested that somehow the knife had sought our family out. Barry marrying Paula may have been more by design than accident — yet Paula wasn't the one the knife was searching for. At that point, I decided that this was far too bizarre. I was simply grateful that the knife had somehow distracted Magnus. All this talk about magic and historical kings was something to ponder at another time and place.

Besides, I had a more important part of my life to consider. His name was Adam. What the two of us had experienced in less than two weeks was far more than many people share in a

lifetime. We were linked on a level so intense that I couldn't imagine ever giving him up.

He told me the same and hinted at a plan to make sure that working in different cities wouldn't put any strain on our love. When I asked what he meant, he simply said, 'Connections.'

★ ★ ★

Later, we were doing an informal debrief with the Tasmanian Police Chief Constable in his office. I was now a guardian of the precious antiquity.

'You do realise that there are some questions that will be asked about your unusual practices while here, Superintendent. We've had reports of a junior officer being coerced into walking around almost naked. There are other serious points that require explanation. In fact, I'm considering a formal report to your superiors — ' His angry lecture was interrupted by the intercom.

'I told you no calls, Kerrie. What

. . . says he's who? Tell him to get lost. Don't bother me again.'

Before he could return to his concerns, his phone rang. 'Who?' he yelled.

The phone was on loud speaker.

'This is the Prime Minister, Chief Constable.'

'I don't think so. First of all, he wouldn't ring me and secondly you don't sound anything like the old bastard. At least you could try to get his voice right. Now push off.'

It was a very controlled voice that responded. I noticed Adam smirking as he sat back.

'Chief Constable. I can see you on your video-link. May I strongly suggest you turn yours on before I contact the Premier about your early retirement?'

'What . . . well, I . . . ' The Chief Constable was about to disconnect when he noted Adam's relaxed attitude. 'Do you know the PM at all, Superintendent?'

'First name terms, Chief Constable.

That's why I asked him to ring us all here. Might I suggest activating the video link? The 'old bastard' doesn't like to be messed around.'

The next ten minutes were a lesson in humility and sycophantic grovelling.

I was pleased to hear that Jill and Mick were to be commended for their actions in apprehending Magnus and her henchmen. The criminal gang would be transferred to a maximum security facility in the Australian Capital Territory to await their trials. It was a very subdued Chief Constable who turned his camera and screen to us.

It was a surprise as well as being a little scary when our country's leader addressed me.

'As for you, DC Ashton, I am informed that you may have some sort of psychic connection to this knife. May I see her?'

Carnwennan was held up to the video link.

'I'm keen to examine her in person,' he went on. 'As are a number of

specialists in Canberra.'

I was unsure what was being proposed.

'Canberra? I thought she was to be returned to Britain?'

'That was the original plan. However discovering the unique bond you share with the knife, I believe that the trip back may be delayed. A mix-up in the paperwork, perhaps? Shall we say a decade or so?' The PM gave me a knowing glance.

'In addition, I'm arranging that you, DC Ashton, are permanently seconded to our Federal Police in Canberra starting in a fortnight. Superintendent Powell and you could have that time together as a holiday — on full pay, of course. I look forward to meeting you in person, Sandie Ashton. We have a lot of work to do together.'

The call was disconnected which was a good thing. It would have been somewhat awkward to contain my joy at the news. Farewell to the problems of that distance between Canberra and

Sydney. My dreams and desires had been answered. Certainly, I had no doubt that it had been Adam's brainwave to remove the one apprehension I'd had about the prospect of our relationship lasting forever.

I didn't care about upsetting the Chief Constable further by kissing in his office and, judging by Adam's equally amorous response, neither did he.

It was time to say goodbye to my lonely life in Sydney. I had a new job by Adam's side. But first a two week stay in my home State, getting to be with my family and my new partner sounded like the perfect start to the year 2000 and our exciting future . . . together.

We do hope that you have enjoyed reading this large print book.

Did you know that all of our titles are available for purchase?

We publish a wide range of high quality large print books including:
Romances, Mysteries, Classics
General Fiction
Non Fiction and Westerns

Special interest titles available in large print are:
The Little Oxford Dictionary
Music Book, Song Book
Hymn Book, Service Book

Also available from us courtesy of Oxford University Press:
Young Readers' Dictionary
(large print edition)
Young Readers' Thesaurus
(large print edition)

For further information or a free brochure, please contact us at:
Ulverscroft Large Print Books Ltd.,
The Green, Bradgate Road, Anstey,
Leicester, LE7 7FU, England.
Tel: (00 44) 0116 236 4325
Fax: (00 44) 0116 234 0205

Other titles in the
Linford Romance Library:

HEARTS AND FLOWERS

Vivien Hampshire

Though her former partner is completely uninterested in his unborn child, heavily pregnant Jess can't wait to meet her new baby. However, she hadn't planned on going into early labour at the local garden centre! After baby Poppy arrives, the manager Ed visits the pair in hospital, and they strike up a friendship. Ed finds himself falling for Jess — but can't quite bring himself to tell her. Will the seeds of their chance encounter eventually blossom into love between them?

WHAT THE HEART WANTS

Suzanne Ross Jones

Alistair is looking for a very particular kind of wife: a country girl who would be happy to settle down to life on his farm in the small town of Shonasbrae. Bonnie, fresh from the city to open her first of many beauty salons, isn't looking for a husband and she certainly isn't accustomed to country life. With such conflicting goals, Alistair and Bonnie couldn't be less compatible. But romance doesn't always make sense, and incompatible as the two are, they don't seem to be able to stay apart . . .

THE JADE TURTLE

Margaret Mounsdon

When Jack and Alice split up, he broke not only her heart, but also their business partnership. Running their agency alone, Alice discovers that Lan Nguyen had, unbeknownst to her, contracted Jack to steal a jade turtle. Unable to refund Lan, Alice is expected to take on the job herself. Reluctant to commit theft, she finds an unexpected ally in Jack's brother Mike. Then somebody else steals the turtle first — and Alice and Mike must find out who!

HER FORGOTTEN LOVE

Elizabeth McGinty

When Elisa catches her partner in bed with another woman, she sets off for Italy to stay with her grandfather Stephano. Greeted at Verona airport by her childhood friend Cesare — now a handsome policeman — she learns that Stephano is ill in hospital, and just manages to see him before he passes away. Then she finds out that he has left her his beloved hotel. Can she make a new life for herself in Italy — perhaps with Cesare by her side?